"Why don't you ge
I'll be right there.

Feeling brave, Mercy reached behind her back and unsnapped her bra, letting it fall to the floor. Her panties were next. Once she was completely naked under the silky sheets, she relaxed.

Will didn't come to bed, however. He went over to the armoire, which was filled with all kinds of adult toys and treats. She held her breath, hoping he wasn't going for something *too* kinky.

Her gaze settled on his cute rear. Whatever Will did to keep in shape sure worked. There wasn't a thing wrong. Not one thing. Well, except that he'd be leaving Hush soon.

This wasn't about forever. It was about tonight. No way was she going to get sentimental.

She was going to have sex. With a gorgeous, nice man.

He turned, treats in hand, and gave her a long, lingering look. Mercy threw back the covers.

It was going to be fantastic....

Blaze™

Dear Reader,

Welcome back to Hush and the DO NOT DISTURB miniseries!

Yes, I had to return one more time to my favorite hotel, only this time, we're hanging out at PetQuarters, the luxury hotel/spa for animals. Something you should know—every pet mentioned in the book, every dog, cat and even fish, is someone's real-life pet. I asked my blog readers to send me pictures and descriptions of their pet's cutest habits and quirks. Each one was cast in a supporting role. Talk about fun!

As adorable as the critters were, it was even more fun to hang out with Mercy Jones and Will Desmond. Mercy is the pet concierge from my March 2008 book, *COMING SOON*, and it's no wonder she got the job. The woman is magic with animals. Not so much with humans, especially male humans. Definitely not with a male of the extreme hotness of Will Desmond. When he walks into her life, what choice does she have but to go for it?

Be sure to visit my blog at www.joleigh.com/wp and see the real pictures of the amazingly adorable pet guest stars!

Love,

Jo Leigh

JO LEIGH
Have Mercy

TORONTO • NEW YORK • LONDON
AMSTERDAM • PARIS • SYDNEY • HAMBURG
STOCKHOLM • ATHENS • TOKYO • MILAN • MADRID
PRAGUE • WARSAW • BUDAPEST • AUCKLAND

ISBN-13: 978-0-373-79402-7
ISBN-10:   0-373-79402-9

HAVE MERCY

This edition published by arrangement with Harlequin Books S.A.

® and TM are trademarks of the publisher. Trademarks indicated with ® are registered in the United States Patent and Trademark Office, the Canadian Trade Marks Office and in other countries.

www.eHarlequin.com

Printed in U.S.A.

ABOUT THE AUTHOR

Jo Leigh has written more than thirty novels for Harlequin and Silhouette books since 1994. She's a triple RITA® finalist, most recently receiving a nomination from the Romance Writers of America for her Blaze novel, *Relentless*. She also teaches writing in workshops across the country.

Jo lives in Utah with her wonderful husband and their cute puppy, Jessie. You can come chat with her at her Web site: www.joleigh.com, and don't forget to check out her daily blog!

Books by Jo Leigh
HARLEQUIN BLAZE

*Men To Do   ‡Forbidden Fantasies
**24 Hours: Island Fling   ‡‡Do Not Disturb
††In Too Deep...

To everyone who shared their pets with me!
You guys are great!

1

AT THIRTY-TWO, Will Desmond had traveled the world, created a successful business and been with beautiful and accomplished women—sometimes simultaneously—but he'd never had a dog. Until now.

Buster, an odd blending of Jack Russell terrier and dachshund, was six months old and ill-behaved, but he was the kind of cute that made women stop in the middle of shopping to stare, to coo. It wouldn't have shocked Will if a mere touch to Buster's little brown head kick-started ovulation. And if attracting women had been his goal, Will would have been a very happy man. But he needed Buster for something else. Something far less pleasant.

Buster, the adorable puppy with the big amber eyes, was Will's shill.

There was still a great deal to discover before the real work would begin. A lot of questions that needed answering. Why Hush, for example.

The hotel was as beautiful as it was controversial. A place no mother would send her daughter. Filled with celebrities, sex and scandal, according to the billboards, the tabloids, the ads in glossy magazines.

He hadn't expected it to be this classy.

Art deco influences led the way to soft, cool luxury. Everything in the lobby was designed to welcome, to make the guest feel special and pampered. Even the staff had that beautiful but not unattainable aura about them, from the concierge to the bartender.

It was a hot spot for the young and wealthy. So what the hell was Drina doing here? Of all the hotels in New York, she'd picked Hush? It didn't add up. Yet.

With Buster in his carrier, Will cruised through the bar, Erotique, liking the soft jazz that played in the background and the way the tables offered a nice place to sit and talk, instead of screaming over rock music. He thought about getting himself a cognac, but he still had to register, and besides, it was only five-thirty, and he hadn't had dinner.

Instead, he studied the clientele. There wasn't a slacker in the bunch. Designer labels, two-hundred-dollar haircuts, high-paying jobs. There were more Rolexes per table than he'd seen since he'd stayed at the Pierre. Although this crowd was a lot younger.

There'd been a big article about Hush in the papers a couple of months ago. A paparazzo had been murdered in the basement nightclub and a film mogul had gone down, but Will couldn't remember the details. He'd have to look it up. What he did remember was reading about the amenities that came with every room. An armoire filled with sex toys, costumes, videos. Everything a true hedonist could wish for, and then some. Too bad he was here on business.

It was time to check in. Behind the glossy ebony reservation desk were two attractive staffers, both wearing the signature black tuxedos with pink bow ties. The pink neon Hush on the wall behind them looked surpris-

get his key, to get directions to PetQuarters, the hotel within the hotel that catered to pampered pets, and to pry Buster away from not only Charlene, but also Kennedy, Blake and Mia, all of whom were equally attractive and bedazzled by the mighty power of the adorable puppy.

Finally, it was just him, Buster and his rolling luggage in the elevator, along with a couple of worker bees from Dynatech who, from the looks of things, couldn't wait to jump each other's bones. But they got off on eight.

The elevator stopped three more times before reaching the fourteenth floor, and it was gratifying that not all of the appreciative glances from the lady passengers were directed at Buster.

He'd have to come back to Hush another time. When he had nothing on his mind but R & R.

Once inside the suite, Hush surprised him yet again. They'd gotten the details just right, from the extravagantly stocked bar to the art deco, to the linens. It wasn't just first class, but five-star.

He recognized the artist of the painting over the hearth. He'd wager it would go for fifty thousand, at least.

Unable to help himself, he opened the legendary armoire in the bedroom. It was a cornucopia of sexual temptations, all neatly packaged and presented with candor. A variety of condoms led the way, with a soupçon of *Kama Sutra* and a bit of leather thrown in for good measure.

If only he'd had someone to share it with, this trip to Hush might not be such a chore. Someone other than Buster.

Closing the armoire, he quickly set up his laptop and did a sweep of his e-mail. All of it could wait, at least until tonight. Then he called down to the front desk.

"Drina Dalakis, please. She's a guest."

"One moment, sir."

He waited, glanced at his watch. The call rang through but he hung up before she could answer.

She was at the hotel, all right. Checked in under her own name. Will bit back a curse as he unpacked his few things, checked out the suite's bathroom, then got out all the paperwork he'd need for PetQuarters.

The dog was whining a bit and even though Will needed to check his phone messages he didn't have much time left before the pet center would close.

"Come on, Buster," he said as he got the carrier from the floor. "Just keep on being adorable, kid, and you and I will get along just fine."

WITH LIGHTNING purring around her neck, Jessie pressed up against her right side, Goober on the left and the Kid on her lap, Mercy Jones was finally ready to start the meeting. It would be brief, as PetQuarters was jumping.

"Here's the deal," she said, one hand scratching

pleased." She looked down into the Kid's face. "And so are our guests."

Her gaze went back to her people. It still felt odd to be in charge. She was used to being the one in the back. The one who did all the work no one wanted to do. And then, just because she happened to be at the animal rescue shelter on that December night…

"Andrew, did you figure out what was going on with the pool?"

"It's fixed. The filter had gotten screwed up, but Lloyd replaced it."

"Great. Anything else we need to discuss while I'm here?"

Alexis, who was a young apprentice, a volunteer who hoped to someday become a pet concierge in her own right, raised her hand.

"Yeah?" Mercy said, switching off her petting hands.

"Be on the lookout for a couple of leashes. Charlie's at it again."

Mercy shook her head. She needed to figure out a way to get Charlie, an otherwise wonderful Lab/bull terrier mix, to stop stealing and hiding anything he took a fancy to. First it was dog bowls. Then chewies, then squeaky toys. One of these days he was going to take the wrong thing from the wrong dog, and it wouldn't be pretty. "Thanks, Alexis. We'll all watch out."

"Mercy, can we talk about the fridge—"

At the mention of the word, half the crew groaned.

Chrissy, who was on permanent staff, put her hands on her hips. "Come on, people. Even the dogs, except for Charlie, don't steal food from each other. If the bag says *Chrissy,* it means *Chrissy.*"

"She's right." Mercy shifted on the big mat, causing Lightning, a gorgeous tabby cat who loved nothing more than masquerading as a scarf, to look up. "You know all of you are welcome to go to the employee canteen on your lunch breaks. I know it's a hike, but the food is so good. You really should leave poor Chrissy's sandwiches alone."

"It's just that her sandwiches are so good," Gilly said, and that comment got a laugh. From everyone but Chrissy.

"Anything else?" Mercy put the Kid on the floor, then extricated herself from beneath her doggy blanket. She didn't even bother to swipe at the hair all over her coat and pants. There was simply no escape.

"I'd be willing to pay if someone, anyone, can figure out how to get Pumpkin to shut up."

That was Lauren, an apprentice.

Mercy saw she was smiling. Kind of. That wouldn't do. "Pumpkin is just one of those pooches," she said. "Chihuahuas are highly strung, nervous dogs. The only power they have is their bark. But there's something you can try, Lauren. You can go in with her, in her suite, and with some patience and a real sense of calm, Pumpkin might surprise you. I'm betting she'll respond to an air

lesson.

"I'll give it a try," she said, her smile still a bit rueful.

"Great. Let me know how it works out."

"Mercy, come to the front desk, please."

The call over the PetQuarters loudspeaker, which actually wasn't very loud, finished the meeting, which was all right with Mercy. Dogs needed walking, grooming, massages, playtime. There were still about fifteen minutes to go until the front desk would shut down to new guests, but that only heralded the beginning of night service for all their overnight pets. Never a dull moment at PetQuarters.

With Lightning purring in her ear, Mercy went to the front desk, which was separated from the main facility by a big door with a No Admittance warning. The desk itself was where the human business of PetQuarters took place. Retail sales of highly overpriced, brand name pet toys and treats. Videos, training books, all manner of items the wealthy denizens of Hush could buy were always at the ready. Behind the desk was the schedule of dogs and workers, the computer files, the dossiers on each and every pet. It was a large enterprise, and because of Mercy, getting larger each day.

Once she'd closed the door behind her, Mercy saw why she'd been called. Mrs. Kenin, Chance's mom, was waiting, and she didn't look happy.

Mercy's throat tightened and her hand went to Lightning's soft fur. "Hello, Mrs. Kenin."

"Miss Smith, is it?"

"Jones."

"Yes, well. Chance was very upset last night. He didn't sleep at all well, and he piddled where he shouldn't have."

Mercy loved her job more than anything in the world. All except this part. Give her the biggest, roughest, toughest dog in the world, and Mercy would find a way to its heart, but people? Guests? That was what she dreaded.

She'd warned them. Piper Devon, the hotel's owner, Janice Foster, the GM. Mercy had been completely honest from the beginning, letting them know that her people skills pretty much sucked. But they'd assured her she'd learn. She'd become as skilled with the people as she was with their pets. So far, it hadn't worked out very well.

"I'm sorry to hear that," she said. "I'm going to get Gilly. She was watching Chance yesterday and if something happened, she'll know."

Her about-face was quick enough that Mrs. Kenin's objections were cut off by the door. Gilly, Mercy's closest friend, was wonderful with the guests. She'd handle the situation with grace and aplomb.

Gilly was busy, of course. She was mopping the small dog pen. Chance, a very spoiled Lhasa Apso, was on a comfy pillow, happily chewing on a stuffed mouse.

After Mercy filled Gilly in, they swapped places.

Mercy much preferred mopping up pee to appeasing a

animal destination for those who lived and worked in midtown Manhattan, and not just as a pet hotel for those who stayed at Hush.

Soon, perhaps even this year, there would be enough profit to warrant the expansion into the building next door. And that would mean that Mercy would earn her bonus. And *that* would mean she could finally move out of the hellhole of her apartment, a notion that was becoming more and more urgent as each day passed.

WILL MADE IT TO PetQuarters in the nick of time. There was a young man behind the desk who looked up from the computer as Will stepped inside. It was just a front office with some retail space. He couldn't see any of the other animal guests, which wouldn't do.

"May I help you, sir?"

"Will Desmond, here to check Buster in."

"Yes, we have your registration."

For the next several minutes, Will filled out forms as the kid, name of Andrew, checked over Buster's bona fides. There was a lot to make up, as Buster had been acquired just this afternoon, but he didn't think he'd set up any red flags.

"He'll be fine, Mr. Desmond," Andrew said, after the last paper had been signed. "There's plenty for him to do, and lots of friends to play with."

Will moved the carrier slightly back. "I'd like to speak to the concierge, if you don't mind."

Andrew didn't let the request alter his Hush smile. "Of course." He picked up the phone, pressed a button. "Mercy, could you come to the front desk, please."

Will looked at all the pet goodies while he waited, determined to get into the back room. Now would be a good time. They were getting ready to close the doors, which meant that staff would be busy, careless perhaps. He'd make sure to take his time, to see everything he possibly could.

The inner door opened. A young woman stepped up to the desk, and while she wasn't the most beautiful of the staff he'd seen today, there was something about her that had his immediate attention.

Mercy Jones, according to her gold nametag. Pet Concierge. She looked to be in her late twenties, with long, straight blond hair, wispy bangs over her forehead and slightly frightened green eyes.

Frightened. Why? Did she know who he was? Had Drina warned her?

Andrew introduced him, but something told Will not to attempt to shake her hand. He hadn't imagined it, the woman was nervous.

Then she saw the pet carrier with Buster inside and her demeanor changed. Her slender shoulders relaxed, her generous lips formed a slight smile. She moved toward Buster with a confidence that had been completely lacking only seconds ago.

"How can I help you, Mr. Desmond?"

such obvious issues, but for his purposes, she was absolutely ideal. "I—"

"You are the concierge, yes?"

She smiled. "I'd be happy to show you around. Let's get Buster out of that cage first, shall we?"

He nodded, knowing she was going to use Buster as a sort of safety blanket when showing him around. He'd seen the behavior before, and he considered it one of his great strengths that he could size up a character quickly and, for the most part, accurately. He wondered about Mercy's story, although whatever it was, it didn't matter. He'd get what he wanted and then he'd be gone. Since he wasn't going to keep Buster, he'd never return to Pet-Quarters.

After a few moments where she held Buster up to lick her face, she tucked the pup into the cradle of her arm, then lifted the hinged desk, giving Will access. He saw it could be locked from underneath with an old-fashioned safety lock. That was in addition to the lock on the front door.

Mercy held the inner door for him, and he entered a world of color, movement and odor. Not that the odor was necessarily bad, just definitely canine in nature. Canine and antiseptic.

"This is the main floor," Mercy said, petting Buster in a way that had the dog completely at ease. "The three pens are for group play. We separate the dogs by size and temperament groups. You'll never have to worry about Buster getting into too much trouble. Our goal is to wear out the pups with vigorous play, long walks and socialization."

He'd give her one thing—despite her discomfort, she didn't skimp on the tour. He met half a dozen staff members, all wearing black jeans, black lab coats with a pink *Hush* embroidered on the lapels and pink satin bow ties. Most of them wore black Hush baseball caps.

Mercy was the only one whose bow tie had tiny black dogs printed on the pink satin. He wondered if that was something management had thought up, or if it was her own touch. If he had to bet, it would be on Mercy. Just watching her with the animals told him more about her than she'd probably be comfortable with.

Her voice didn't quaver and her step, now that she was inside, was confident, but there was a story there, and not a pleasant one. She'd found herself a refuge, though. One with a lot of wagging tails.

They went to the pet suites in the back of the main room, and he focused once more on business. Mercy might be interesting, but she was a bit player. The star was here. Somewhere. There was no other reason for Drina to have come here with a dog of her own. Drina, who was about as fond of dogs as he was of spiders.

They passed a yapping Chihuahua that looked more like a rat than a dog, a German shepherd, several dogs who looked like mutts to his untrained eyes, and then he saw it. A little dog, one with a great deal of white

2

MERCY KEPT HER eyes peeled for Gilly as she showed Mr. Desmond—Will—the pet suites. It was a good thing for him that he'd made a reservation as all the suites had been booked. That was one of the things that would change when they took over the building next door. They would triple the number of pet suites, add another grooming salon and so much more.

"These are nicer than some hotels I've stayed in," Will said. He was standing in the currently unoccupied Southwestern suite. Each pen was its own room, complete with a twin bed, TV, piped-in music, food and water station, toys and, if a guest so desired, blankets and trinkets brought from home.

"They've all got themes," she said, "although that's more for the parents than the pets."

"I can tell Buster's going to be spoiled."

"We discipline the dogs, gently, of course. We believe strongly in rewarding good behavior."

"You're going to have to be extra gentle with Buster. He's had no training."

"Oh? How long have you had him?"

"Not long. He's a gift for my nephew back in Wichita. I'm taking him with me when I head back home. Cory's birthday is coming up and he's been

Buddhist in a past life. He calmed everyone down, including the most high-strung of the dogs.

Gilly glanced her way. Mercy waved her over, but all Gilly did was smile and go back to tugging on Rio's toy.

Damn her. Gilly knew Mercy hated giving the tours. This one was especially hard because Mr. Desmond was, well, gorgeous.

He was tall, maybe six-two, with dark, thick hair, dark eyes, dark lashes. He was as trim and toned as an athlete, and if she'd been someone else, someone who wasn't a total and complete coward, she'd have asked him what he did for a living. She knew he was successful. He wouldn't be staying at Hush if he wasn't. But that didn't tell her much.

"What about food?"

It took her a few seconds to realize he was talking about Buster. "I'll show you," she said. The meal room was near her office. She led the way, wishing like anything that she didn't feel so awkward. She kept thinking about all the dog hair that was stuck to her jacket and pants, about Mr. Desmond's eyes, about the fact that he wore no wedding band, and how a man like him would never look at a woman with dog hair all over her.

She opened the door and Will stepped inside. She let him take it all in—the refrigerator, the different food formulas for every kind of nutritional need, how spotless everything was.

"Nice," he said. "What is Buster going to eat?"

She told him about the puppy food, and how often Buster would eat. And she told him he'd be able to order the food from Hush if he wanted. They shipped all over the world.

Will looked at her, nothing dramatic, not even really a stare, but it was enough to ignite her blush. Her curse. She blushed at everything, always had. At least when she was talking about PetQuarters, she could lose herself in the canned speeches.

"What brought you here?" he asked. "Before this week, I didn't know there was such a thing as a pet concierge."

"It's a new field, but I've been working with animals since I was sixteen. I met Ms. Devon when I volunteered at an animal rescue shelter. She's very fond of pets and wanted to make sure that no guest would have to leave their critters at home."

"Piper Devon."

"That's right."

He looked back into the main room. "It seems to be going well."

"Very. We're expanding our role, catering not only to registered guests, but pet owners in midtown. We have a lot of daily visitors. Quite a few have already been picked up, but our clientele know we can accommodate crazy schedules."

"So someone's always here."

"Oh, yes. We have night teams. The dogs are mostly

worn out by nightfall, but there's always at least two of us standing by in case of emergency."

"Good to know." He stepped outside the food room just as Emily and Matt came in. Dinner was in half an hour, and even with that much notice the two of them would have to hustle. So many of the pets were on special diets.

"What's back there?" he asked, pointing toward the grooming salon.

"That's where the pampering takes place. We offer any number of grooming options, from a simple bath to dog show prep."

"I noticed you offer pedicures."

She nodded, making sure she didn't roll her eyes. "Everything a pet could ever want."

"Yeah. I'm sure the dogs line up."

"Well, no, but a lot of these pets are like children to their owners."

Will shook his head. "Damn foolish, if you ask me."

"We also offer rehabilitation services. We have a pool for our arthritic guests and we have an acupuncturist here on Mondays, a chiropractor on Wednesdays and we also do wellness checkups given by a really wonderful vet."

"Sounds like you've got everything covered."

"We do. Including walks to the park, unstructured playtime and one-on-one attention from the staff for at least a half hour a day."

He'd wandered back to the suites, standing outside Lulu's room. The dog was already on her little bed waiting for her dinner. Lulu, with the painted toenails and daily grooming, not to mention a collar that was worth more than Mercy would earn in three years.

A yelp made Mercy spin to the middle-dog pen. She handed Buster over to Will and headed straight for the ruckus.

It was Cooper, the Belgian shepherd, who had a lot to learn about playing well with others. She went directly into the pen and to Cooper's side. He dropped the bone from his mouth as he looked up at her.

Tobi Wan Kenobi—a lovely beagle/pit bull—sat down, the bone he'd wanted so badly a moment ago forgotten in his attempt to please Mercy.

She didn't scold Cooper or Tobi, but she did make sure that they were calm and happy before she left them to play in the pen. No one got hurt, no feathers were ruffled. It might be after six but the middle-size dogs were going to get another run tonight, in fact, as soon as she got rid of Will Desmond.

For his part, Mr. Desmond didn't appear to be in any hurry. He was still outside Lulu's suite, leaning against the door, his arms crossed comfortably over his chest.

Talk about a pack leader. Whatever he did in Wichita, he was good at it. She wouldn't be surprised if he ran a great big company, like an airline or a restaurant chain. He exuded that kind of power, the kind where everyone around him put on their nicest clothing in the hopes he'd notice.

Which also meant he got all the girls. All the beauties. She couldn't see him settling for second best. Not with something as important as status.

"How'd you do that?"

"Pardon me?"

"You didn't say anything. I didn't even catch a hand signal. But both those dogs straightened up in a heartbeat."

"Oh. Well, they know I'm the pack leader."

He didn't say anything for a long minute, then he smiled. As he did so his dimples made their debut. Two of them, one on each cheek. They were real dimples, too. Big ones that gave his smile resonance, that changed him from the man you wouldn't dare cross to the man you wanted as your best friend.

It wasn't in the least bit fair. Sort of like Audrey Hepburn or Angelina Jolie. Not only were they stunningly gorgeous, but they were gorgeous actresses as well. Wouldn't it have been nicer if they each got one fabulous gift and spread the wealth?

"I think Buster's going to be very happy here," he said.

"I'm glad you think so. Is there anything else I can help you with?"

"I—"

"Mercy, could you come to the front office, please?" It was the loudspeaker. "I'm sorry, I have to—"

"Ms. Jones!"

Mercy spun around at her name, said so harshly it could only be one of the pet owners. Ah, there she was, standing near the door. Mercy couldn't remember her name, just that she belonged to Pumpkin, the nervous and insistent Chihuahua.

Mercy headed toward the confrontation, wishing she could teach some of the owners about misplaced aggression and how to behave.

"Ms. Jones." The woman was older, maybe in her sixties, had an accent Mercy couldn't identify and she was striking. Beautiful, really. Her hair was silver and sleek, cut in a style that should have been too young for her, but wasn't. She dressed young, too. A nice pair of green pants, a white blouse with a lifted collar. She had nice jewelry, too. Nice as in expensive. "I was supposed to get a phone call this afternoon about Pumpkin's massage."

"I'm so sorry. Was there something in particular you wanted to know?"

"She was limping last night. Something happened here that hurt her leg."

"Why don't we go check on her now?"

The woman sighed, then nodded curtly.

When Mercy turned around, Will Desmond was nowhere to be seen. He might have decided to go exploring on his own, which wasn't good, but then Gilly wasn't around, either. The rat. She'd probably absconded with Desmond, taken him somewhere intimate and private.

Pumpkin's mother followed Mercy to the suite, where Pumpkin greeted them with ferocious barking from atop her bed. Mercy opened the door and went inside. Surprisingly, Pumpkin's mother didn't. It took several minutes to calm the little tan dog down, but finally it was quiet again. Mercy was able to put Pumpkin on the floor. She proceeded to walk around, and there was no sign of a limp.

"She seems to be doing well."

"I suppose so. But I still should have gotten a call."

"Yes, you should have. I'll look in to it and find out what happened. I'm sorry."

Without a move to touch her dog, the woman turned toward the door. She took a step, then stopped. "I'm going out tonight, so you can keep her here. I'll look in on her tomorrow."

"I'll keep my eye on her."

The woman nodded once more, but instead of heading straight to the exit, she wandered down the line of suites. Finally, after looking at all the dogs, she made her way across the room and let herself out.

Mercy picked Pumpkin up. The dog trembled, but didn't bark. After a few minutes of gentle petting, Pumpkin settled and seemed to enjoy the contact.

Something was off between owner and pet, but that wasn't unheard of. "Poor little thing," she whispered. "We'll play tomorrow, you and me. We'll get to know each other better."

Mercy put her down, then left the suite, only to be surprised by Will Desmond. He stood just a few feet away, watching her. Mercy closed the door behind her, then turned to him. "Was there something else?"

He nodded. "I'd like to sign up to have you help me train Buster."

She shook her head. "That's the one thing we don't do. Not yet, at least. But I can give you several referrals who are excellent."

"No. I want you."

The words, even in their proper context, made Mercy flush. For a split second she pretended—but then it was over and she walked to Buster's suite to look in on the pup. He'd piddled on the floor and he'd found a long, stuffed dog to play with. He seemed content, not at all frightened. That was a good thing. "I'm sorry. I don't train dogs."

"You should. You're amazing with them."

"I respect them. I don't see them as little furry humans."

"So bend the rules. For Buster."

"I'm sorry. When you come back tomorrow, I'll have the referrals ready. I really have to get going now."

Instead of turning around, instead of leaving, he moved closer. So close she could see the slight shadow of his beard, the hint of his dimples even with his face in repose. He was too good-looking by far. She stepped back.

"At least consider it," he said. "I'll make it worth your while."

She couldn't move farther back even though his nearness was too much. Was that his cologne she smelled? No, it was too subtle. Soap. That was it. Her gaze shifted down but the dark smattering of hair on his arms teased her. Made her think of other parts of his body.

"I have work—"

"I know. I've overstayed my welcome. I'll leave you, for now. Just please, think about it."

She nodded.

"You're lovely," he whispered.

The slow simmer of blush that had filled her cheeks burst into a heat that burned. She didn't care if he left or not. She was out of there.

Behind her, as she hurried to the grooming salon, she heard his measured footsteps. It was only when she was safe with a door and a room between them that she felt the trembling, immediately followed by a hot surge of humiliation. She was twenty-seven years old, and she still was a complete idiot when it came to men. Not that she was completely inexperienced, but then, none of her experiences had been very good.

She'd missed out on the whole flirting thing. For that matter, she'd never really dated, not like normal girls had. In the end, it was just easier to be with the animals. At least there, she knew just where she stood.

"GET ON TAYLOR'S case first thing in the morning," Will said as he logged into his laptop. "That delivery should have been made yesterday."

"Got it," Anita said. She moved on to the next order of business in her usual professional manner.

Anita had been his administrative assistant for three years, and she was damn good at her job. She kept the distractions to a minimum and while they were friendly, she didn't bother him with her personal life, or expect to know about his.

He'd formed the company eleven years ago, when he'd seen the signs that corporate wellness was going to become a matter of necessity. WD Fitness Equipment designed health facilities for businesses across the country. He had a great team working for him, but he was still the man in charge, and taking any time away from work was costly.

"I've made your reservations for the trade show in Paris. You'll be leaving on the twenty-first."

"Fine. Where are we with the end-of-month numbers?"

He listened as he glanced at the e-mails, at least sixty, waiting for him, then clicked over to Google. After typing in "diamond dog collar" he was surprised to find so many hits.

Anita said something that he made her repeat. When she was finished, he wrapped things up, anxious to get to his personal business.

"Will you be coming in tomorrow?"

"I'll see. I might be able to come in around ten, but don't make any appointments."

He heard a phone ring in the background, and let Anita go. The office wasn't far, just across town in

SoHo, but until he knew exactly what was going on with Drina, he didn't want to leave the hotel.

He went back to his online search, running down the list of hits. Although he didn't see many links to diamond dog collars made recently, there had been several in the news from the 1920s. Evidently, diamonds on dog collars had been in vogue, and several well-known socialites had spent hundreds of thousands of dollars to upstage their neighbors.

There were a few pictures, and one of them looked a lot like the collar he'd seen on Lulu. He'd call an old friend of his, a P.I. from Jersey, and get him to look into the possibility that the collar had been purchased at auction or if the transaction had made the news. He wished he could have turned this whole mess over to Ricky, but the matter required his personal attention. So while Ricky did the research, Will would do some digging the old-fashioned way—by getting someone to talk.

Not someone. Mercy.

He wondered again about her story. She really was lovely. Tall, slender but not ridiculously so, she reminded him of a colt. Skittish and headstrong, it would be a challenge to get past her defenses. But worth it, he thought. Not just because she would know about the collar, either.

He wasn't sure how long it was going to take to get to the bottom of things here, but he wasn't quite as anxious as he'd been this morning.

Mercy had been clear that she wasn't going to help him train Buster. Will smiled as he recalled her delectable pout. He'd always liked a challenge, especially when the reward was so tempting.

3

THE HUSH ROOFTOP garden was as lush with fragrance as it was with beauty. Drina had found a small wooden table under a shade tree where she could drink her mimosa and stare at her still-empty journal. She closed her eyes as a warm humid breeze caressed her face, wishing as always that Marius could be with her.

If Marius had still been alive he would have approved. Her duty was to make sure the bastards paid for what they'd done. To catch them at the perfect moment and expose them for the thieves they were.

After another sip of her drink she picked up the pen that had been her husband's. It was silver and it had once had the name of a stranger engraved on the top, but now there was no name, only the memory of her beautiful Marius…and how she missed his touch.

She put the pen to the paper, marking down the date, the weather, the scent of roses. And then she went back in time, to before she was born. The stories of how the family had come to America were more vivid to her than the television show she'd watched last night.

All her life the old ones had repeated the tales, had sat the children around the tables and gone through the litany of trials they'd faced while keeping each other

safe, always begun and ended with the dangers of as-
similation. They were separate. They were special. No
one was safe outside the circle of family.

She wrote quickly, not lifting the pen for a page,
then two, as she remembered her mother. She'd been
fourteen when she'd come to New York, already married
and pregnant with Drina's eldest brother. The trip over
on the boat had nearly cost Stefan his new life, but once
Mama had gone to New Jersey with Papa, he'd flour-
ished.

The family had grown with uncles, aunts, cousins.
They worked together, lived together. Drina had spoken
the old language until she'd been forced to go to school.
It had been a horrible time for her. Strangers, strange
ways. The other children laughed at her Romanian
accent, at her lunches, at her hand-me-down clothes.

It didn't matter. The family was everything, and from
the time she could walk she'd been in training.

In her family, the girls were treated no differently
from the boys except that they learned early to use their
sex. Not that way. That was what the outsiders believed,
but in her family, they raised good girls. Good girls
who were expert pickpockets and who understood how
to work the con.

She'd been pure until the day she'd married Marius.
How she'd wanted him. He was the best-looking boy
she'd ever seen. The moment they'd met, she'd known
they would be together. Forever.

They would have still been together if it hadn't
been—

The ding of the elevator made her look up, forget-
ting for a moment where she was. A blink later she re-

membered why she was here, and that she had to be careful.

She closed the memory book, finished the rest of her drink. Then sat back in the shadows to wait. To see if they kept to their schedule. To see the bastards who'd sent her Marius to prison and to his death.

Five minutes passed with nothing but the breeze to stir the air. She thought of Dennis, her current gentleman friend. He was pleasant, a decent man, but just another distraction. As she waited, she wondered again why she bothered. The only thing that mattered in her life was this. Was revenge.

Another two minutes, and she wished she hadn't finished her drink. Then a sound.

She waited, knowing she would see them as they walked the dog, but that they couldn't see her. Knowing they wouldn't leave the path. They were predictable and that made them fools.

This dog, unlike the annoying Pumpkin, didn't bark. But it did make enough noise that Drina was able to back up even farther before she saw them.

The diamonds in the collar glittered in the sun but Drina's eyes narrowed for another reason. The two of them—her holding the leash, him with his hand in his pockets—walked through the garden as if they weren't evil. As if they'd never betrayed the family. Never spit on the memory of their ancestors.

They wouldn't gloat for long. Soon, they would be sorry. They would curse the day they'd turned on Marius, and they would have the rest of their lives to think about their sins. The dog was the key.

Fools. Did they imagine she needed Marius to figure

out their con? Drina had known from the first. It had taken strength and perseverance to figure out their plan, but she'd been trained by the best. She would have her revenge and it would taste like her husband's kiss.

FOUR DOGS, each of them over seventy pounds, walked behind Mercy in polite formation, undistracted by the pedestrians, the cars, the scents of Madison Avenue. They knew they were heading for the park, and the park meant rolling in the grass, sniffing all manner of things, running like mad.

Gilly had four dogs of her own, not as large as Mercy's group but just as well-behaved. The two women couldn't walk next to each other as they would have owned the whole street, but they still managed to talk.

This morning's walk, there was only one topic. Will Desmond.

"He was totally flirting with you," Gilly said. "I was across the room and I saw it."

"He was trying to get me to help train his dog."

"That was his excuse, Mercy. He wants you."

Mercy laughed. "Yeah, right. Did you look at him?"

"The more important question is have you looked at you?"

"I have," she said. "I've even had dinner with me, and I'll tell you right now, a man like Will Desmond is as interested in me as he is a toaster."

"Wrong, wrong, wrong. He couldn't keep his eyes off you."

"Gilly, don't be absurd." They turned the corner, and her dogs got a bit excited, lunging forward. They all knew the route to the park, and they wanted to be there now. She corrected the behavior and like the good puppies they were, they eased back into contented pack mode.

Gilly followed suit with her group.

Gilly had already been at Hush when Mercy had gotten the job. She'd been a cocktail waitress at Exhibit A, the downstairs club that had been the sight of the recent scandal, but she'd hated the work. She'd taken a huge pay cut, but Gilly had a real affinity for the animals.

Mercy had liked her from the first day, and while she'd never had a lot of friends, she and Gilly had grown closer and closer as they'd worked side-by-side.

Mercy loved that Gilly was so open and friendly, although it probably would have worked out better for both of them if Gilly would stop trying to fix her up.

Although she was as honest as she could be with Gilly, she hadn't been able to tell her a lot about her past. A person doesn't just come out with that kind of stuff after a lifetime of holding it in. Gilly didn't understand that Mercy hadn't lived the kind of suburban, middle-class life that included boys and dating and sock hops or whatever the hell people did in the suburbs.

"When's the last time you went out?"

Mercy sighed. "Gilly, let it go."

"No. I won't. You haven't been out with a guy in a hundred years."

"That's true. And it'll be another hundred until the next one."

"Mercy!"

"I'm not pursuing this. It's ridiculous. The man is

so far out of my league he's in another dimension, so let it go."

"What if he isn't? What if I'm right and he was hitting on you?"

"So?"

They stopped at the street corner, Gilly moving up so that all the dogs were lined up as if they were going to race. Mercy ignored the evil glances from their fellow pedestrians. Normally, she'd have pulled back, but the light was going to change in a hot second.

"Let's make this hypothetical."

"No. Let's not."

Gilly glared her way, then went on as if Mercy hadn't said a word. "Let's say Will thought you were hot. That he asked you to help train Buster as a way of getting to know you."

"Gil—"

The light turned green and the team crossed the street in a frenzy of sniffing and lurching. They were too close to the park to be having this stupid conversation.

"Let's say that you agreed to help him train the dog. And you agreed to do it in his suite. Which is suite fourteen-twelve, by the way, one of the really, really expensive suites."

"I'm not listening."

"You are so. Anyway, you go up to his room. Get Buster to sit. Will pulls you into his arms for a bone-melting kiss—"

"Gilly, stop."

"You tear off each other's clothes and go at it like poodles. You're happy and exhausted. He's happy and exhausted. Buster knows how to sit on command. What's so terrible about that?"

"Aside from the fact that he's a guest?"

"In your case, we can make an exception. I think I saw it in the employee's handbook. Anyone who hasn't been laid in a year gets to screw any guest they want to."

Mercy looked at her ex-friend. "Gee, next time, maybe you can have that printed on a T-shirt so everyone would know."

"No one on this street cares if you've gotten laid."

"I do."

Mercy jerked around to see a grinning homeless man standing a few inches away.

She scowled at Gilly and speeded up.

Gilly laughed so hard the dogs got scared. Not that she cared. Gilly was one of those people who walked through life as if it was her playground. She didn't get scared, didn't blush, and when she made a fool of herself she shrugged it off with such ease it made Mercy cry from envy.

It didn't hurt that she was pretty, either. Tall, voluptuous, with dark curly hair that framed her face and made her look a hell of a lot more innocent than she was. Gilly also had a fabulous boyfriend, Gordon, who was a concierge at the Muse.

The park was just across the street, and while they waited to cross there was no use even trying to talk. All focus was on the dogs, who were salivating to go inside the fenced-in doggie area and run around in the grass.

It was always a joy to take off their leashes, to see them grin their puppy grins as they darted into the thick of things. Today, the dog park was a little crowded, but there was still an empty bench, which she and Gilly snagged.

"The great thing about him is that he's leaving," Gilly said as she wrapped her leashes into a big roll.

"He's a guest."

"He's leaving. You know how people are when they check in to Hush. He's got that whole chest of toys just sitting there, calling him. What's the worst thing that could happen?"

"I get fired."

"Come on. That's never gonna happen. Piper loves you. She'd never fire you."

"If I'm caught, what choice would she have?"

"You won't get caught."

Mercy smiled. "That's right. Because I'm not going to do it."

Gilly shook her head. "You're too smart to let this opportunity get away from you. He's gorgeous, he's horny, he's leaving. It's a gift, Mercy. You just have to unwrap it and it's yours."

"I just have to take care of the pets," she said.

Gilly's look was meant to urge her on, but all Mercy felt was pathetic. She should never have talked to any of them about her personal life. Hadn't she learned by now to keep her big mouth shut?

"Maybe it's okay, once every five years or so, to take care of yourself. The animals are great, Mercy, but they're not a substitute for love."

"Love?" Mercy snorted. "Come on—"

"Okay, so maybe not love, but how about human companionship? How about comfort? People need contact. It's how we're designed, and you're no different."

"I've had all the contact I need."

"No, you haven't. Besides, if it gets you out of your apartment for a night…"

"That's the first thing you've said that makes any sense."

"See? I knew you'd come around. Now, we just have to make sure Gorgeous Will comes back to visit Buster—"

Mercy slugged her friend in the shoulder, which did shut her up. But it wouldn't stop her from plotting and planning. It's what Gilly did best.

IT WAS JUST PAST six when Will found himself an empty stool at Erotique, the Hush bar. He'd tried, with no success, to change Mercy's mind about training Buster, and with that defeat he'd realized he'd have to take another tack.

"Glenfiddich," he said to the bartender.

"I've got the single malt or the special reserve."

"Single malt."

The bartender, a tall guy who was undoubtedly working here until he got his big break on Broadway, went off to fetch the scotch and Will turned to case the room. The bar was just starting to fill with the after-work crowd, and he was once again amazed at the obvious signs of wealth. This place was a treasure trove of watches, diamond rings, laptops, iPhones and electronic gear of every stripe. Even the briefcases were polished leather and monogrammed, of course.

And the women were all beautiful. Even if they hadn't been born that way, they used every trick in the book to appear as if their good looks were nothing special. He wondered how many cosmetic surgeons were sending their kids to Harvard from this crowd alone.

He was one of the lucky ones. He'd been born with his grandfather's dark handsomeness, and he'd learned early not to squander the gift. It had made so much of life so much easier.

Women had never been a problem, and even in business, people were more likely to part with money if the person asking had a symmetrical, pleasing face and body.

Personally, he never understood why so many people didn't clue in to the beauty factor. It was just a fact of human nature, not good, not bad. Simply useful.

"Here you go, sir," the bartender said. "Can I get you anything else?"

Will pulled a folded hundred out of his jacket pocket and discreetly pushed it into the young man's hand. "Tell me something, Karl. What do you know about Mercy Jones?"

"Mercy…oh, you mean the pet concierge."

Will nodded before taking his first sip. The scotch was unbelievably smooth, and he savored the slow, subtle burn.

"Let's see." Karl picked up a glass and a cloth, and proceeded to use one on the other. "She's one of Ms. Devon's projects. Found her in a shelter."

"I heard she worked for animal rescue?"

"Yeah. But she was something of a rescue herself, although that's all rumor. She's the quiet type. About everything. I see her in the cafeteria from time to time, but she keeps to herself."

"Not dating anyone?"

"Not that I've seen. But one of the waitresses knows her. I'll ask."

"Thanks, Karl. I appreciate it."

Karl took a few more orders, but given the size of his tip, Will felt sure he'd find out all he could. And now that that piece of business was in motion, it was time to relax. To appreciate his drink, to think about Drina and the damned diamond dog collar.

Drina, he surmised, was going to steal the thing. Fine. What he couldn't figure out, however, was what she was planning to do with it, after she had it. The collar was undoubtedly insured, and since it was such an unusual piece, the police would notice if it suddenly came on the market. He doubted any reputable fence would take the thing, at least not for a few years.

Besides, it wasn't a smart move. That made him more uncomfortable than anything else. Drina was not a stupid woman, and she didn't make big mistakes. Was she losing it? Or was there something about this collar that he hadn't discovered yet?

His money was on the latter.

"Mr. Desmond?"

So Karl had gotten his name. Smart kid.

"Mercy doesn't have a boyfriend, no. She spends all her time at PetQuarters."

Will bit back a smile as Karl leaned in and told his tale as if he was spilling the beans to Jason Bourne. All very hush-hush.

"She's very tight with Gilly, who works with her, but that's about it. Word is she's doing everything she can to get her big bonus so that she can move to a place of her own."

"Big bonus?"

He nodded. "She's trying to get enough day business so Piper will turn the building next door into a huge pet facility. If Mercy does it, brings in enough revenue, she gets a bonus. I'm not sure how much, but I can probably find out."

"No, that's fine, Karl, thank you."

"Sure thing." The young man smiled and turned to help his other customers.

Just before he was out of earshot, Will said, "Karl, one more thing."

"Sir?"

"You know anything about that crazy dog collar? It's a fake, right? It has to be a fake."

Karl shook his head. "Oh, no, sir. It's no fake. Everyone knows about the diamond collar. It was even in the paper. It's worth, I don't know, almost a million dollars. At least, that's what I heard. Can you imagine? Putting that kind of money on a dog?"

"Well, I'll be damned. I never would have guessed."

"You'd be surprised the kind of crazy stuff that goes on in a hotel like this. I could tell you stories—"

"I'll bet you could. Tell you what, though. Let's refill this glass, first."

Karl nodded and headed for the bottle.

Will got comfortable. He probably wouldn't learn anything useful from Karl's tales of hotel life, but it was worth listening nonetheless. It wouldn't hurt to get an insider's view, and besides, he'd learned young not to let any opportunity slip by.

Just the fact that all the employees knew about the collar was something that might come in real handy.

His smile fell as he thought about Mercy. He'd been right about her. She wasn't being coy with those blushes. She'd had enough trouble in her life to want to keep it to herself. That should have made him happy. So much easier to get what he wanted from a woman with big issues. But all he felt was tired.

He wanted to go home. He wanted...

Shit, he didn't even know what he wanted.

4

THE WALK FROM the bus stop to Mercy's apartment was always the scariest, if not the worst, part of going home. She lived in an area of New York that had been taken over by drugs and spiraling unemployment. There were hookers and dealers and gangs and a whole bunch of other things to be worried about every time she stepped off the bus.

But she had the routine down pat. She wore a backpack instead of a purse and kept her money in her shoe. She made herself small, but made sure not to look like a victim. She never ran. Her key was in her hand before she got off the bus, and in her right front pocket she kept a switchblade. Thank goodness she'd never had to use it. At least not while she'd lived here.

This wasn't the first time she'd lived in a scary place. In fact, there hadn't been many nonscary places in her life. Truth be told, she preferred the fear to be on the outside of the house. It was easier to sleep that way.

She made it the six blocks to her apartment building without incident, even in the four floors up to her door. As usual, it smelled like a pit in the stairwells, and sounded just as bad, but there were no junkies lurking.

She unbolted the door, stepped inside and tried not

to look around. It would just depress her more to see the squalor she lived in.

She had a minimum of four roommates. Sometimes six, depending on who needed a place to crash and who was desperate for money. The whole place was just over four hundred square feet. One bathroom, a micro-kitchen that had a half fridge, a hot plate and an oven that never worked. There were three couches in the main room, usually doubling as beds.

Her room, the only slightly serene place to be found, had been a closet. It now held all her earthly posses-sions, most of them folded in stacked milk crates she'd painted blue.

Her bed was a single mattress on the floor. The walls of her closet were pale blue, too, and the best thing was she actually had a window. It was small, too high to see out unless she climbed on a chair, but sometimes when she was there in the daytime, the sun hit the end of the bed.

All this, including the fact that she had to dead-bolt herself inside the closet before she went to sleep, for just under nine hundred per month.

It all would have been tolerable if she'd been able to share the space with a dog, or even a cat. But there were no pets allowed. For her that meant no joy allowed.

She'd been spending the night at Hush so often she was afraid someone was going to tell the GM, and they'd tell her to stop. Even though she worked when she was there overnight, she still slept better, felt safer. She'd even thought, briefly, of asking if she could move in to PetQuarters permanently. Well, until she got her bonus.

That ten thousand dollars was going to free her.

She'd find another apartment, with a maximum of one roommate. And she'd have a dog. Maybe a dog and a cat. Wouldn't that be something?

She got into her sleep shirt, then waited until she heard whoever the hell was in the bathroom leave. She never even bothered to shower there anymore. There was a great staff shower at PetQuarters, thank goodness. But she did brush her teeth, then scurry back to her room.

Inside, she turned on the good light, fixed her pillows and went back to her book. It was an old favorite about a veterinary practice in the English countryside. From her backpack she pulled out a PowerBar and a bottle of water, and waited for the magic.

Books had always been her sacred place. Through years of horrific foster parents and equally horrific state homes, she'd found she could lose herself in two things—books and animals.

However, tonight she couldn't get into the rhythm. She'd read a paragraph, then have to go back and read it again because she had no idea what it said.

Over and over she tried, until she finally surrendered to the thoughts that had plagued her since this afternoon when Will Desmond had come to visit Buster.

She hadn't heard him come in. In fact, she probably wouldn't have noticed him if it hadn't been for Lightning.

The cat was around her neck, as usual. Then, in a trick that had made more than one guest shriek, she'd lifted her head and hissed. At Will.

He'd stepped back, his eyes wide and his body defensive. Mercy had been just as surprised but her defensiveness was for a completely different reason.

She'd been working with Goober, a little Doberman mix, getting him to settle down so he could go into the pen with his buddies. Naturally, Goober started barking, which scared Lightning, who'd jumped down from Mercy's back, leaving a few choice claw marks. Mercy focused on Goober, shushing him and calming him as she tried to calm her own heart.

Will had apologized, but he hadn't left. He'd stayed until Goober was in the pen. Until she'd gotten Buster from his pen and handed him to his Uncle Will.

Even then, even when she went to the grooming room to check on Lulu and Chance, Will and Buster had trailed along.

They'd talked about the facility, about New York, about the different grooming techniques. It seemed to Mercy that he had an unending supply of questions. Finally, when she'd mentioned that he wasn't having much of a vacation, he'd confessed that he came to the city all the time. That he liked the feel of PetQuarters. That he liked the company.

Thank goodness Gilly hadn't heard that. She'd have jumped all over that silly comment. Mercy had dismissed it as nonsense from a lonely traveler, but she hadn't really bought it.

Now, sitting in her crappy little room on her crappy little bed, she faced the truth.

Gorgeous Will, with his dark good looks and his big old dimples, had flirted with her.

Why? She wasn't anything special, and he was. It didn't make sense. It was easy to imagine him with the most amazing women in New York. Hell, she could see him with Piper Devon, and that didn't happen much. Well, especially because Piper was happily married, but still, they would have looked right sitting together at Amuse Bouche, sharing champagne and caviar.

So why was he flirting with her?

Of all the things her life had taught her, the number-one lesson was that people were predictable. They stayed with their own kind. If they had to shift out of their comfort zone, it was almost always because they wanted something.

So what did Will want?

He was staying in a suite, for God's sake, in Hush. That cost a fortune. He'd said he came to the city from Wichita all the time. He was a wealthy, successful guy. Why would he want to slum it with a working stiff like her?

Maybe that was the point. Maybe he was looking for something different, something a little dangerous. Slumming it with her might be his version of a walk on the wild side.

If that were true, he sure as hell had his act down. He'd never made her feel like she was trash. In fact, he'd said a lot of really nice things. Not random things, either. He'd noticed how she handled the dogs. How they all responded to her. He'd commented on the setup in PetQuarters—seen how she'd arranged things to work smoothly and cleanly.

He'd even complimented her on her staff, and man, that had given her a lump in her throat. More than that, the dogs liked him. Not just Buster but all of them. They wagged their tails and eagerly accepted his attentions. Nothing could have convinced her that Will was a decent guy more than that.

Then, just before he left, he'd asked her again to help him train Buster. The dog was such a sweetie that she'd almost said yes.

Okay, that's not why she'd almost said yes. Gilly's words had haunted her since the walk. Will was a guest, a stranger, a visitor. He wasn't going to stick around for long, so how messy could things get?

He wanted her to bring Buster up after hours. So she'd already be in his suite. But anyway, she'd be there, and the bedroom would be right there, and since everyone was kind of used to her spending the night at the hotel…

No. She couldn't. It was too risky, and not just the part about Will being a guest.

She wasn't good with people. With men. She blushed like an infant, she stumbled over her words, she knew squat about etiquette and civilized behavior. It would mean getting naked. That couldn't end well.

On the other hand—

No. There was no other hand. It was only nine-thirty, but Mercy turned off the good light and got under the covers. No way she was going to do anything with Will. His dimples be damned.

WILL WATCHED Drina as she ate her lunch. He was sitting in a far booth, one that was positioned perfectly, allowing him to see her, but keeping her from catching him at it.

He'd ordered some fish and as he waited for the meal to arrive, he simply watched her. Even at her age, she was a beauty. Her hair was silver now, short, classy. Her wardrobe was modern, and yet there was an old-style grace in the loose scarf around her neck.

She was the very picture of a wealthy woman, a woman used to luxury and comfort.

He knew better.

She was a thief of the first order, that one. One of the

best con artists he'd ever seen. Devious, beguiling, charming. She'd never met a person she couldn't con.

Damn it, why couldn't he figure out what she wanted with the collar? There were easier things to steal. Easier things to fence. What was it that had her checking in to Hush? Getting a dog of her own?

He had to get to the bottom of this thing before it went too far. He needed to find out about Lulu's owners. He'd already asked Ricky to do some checking on the insurance angle.

Maybe the owners had hired Drina in order to collect on the insurance? Maybe that collar wasn't as real as the papers would have him believe. Maybe—

His fish came, and with it renewed determination. He was going to ease his way into PetQuarters. Into the confidence of Mercy Jones.

It wasn't an unpleasant assignment. In fact, it was the only bonus in a distasteful situation.

He really liked the way she blushed. There was more to her than that, of course, but it wouldn't do him any good to go there. She was a means to an end. He'd try to leave her with good memories and a smile. That was the best he could offer.

Mercy was his ticket in. Period.

In fact, after lunch, he'd go back to PetQuarters, and this time, he wouldn't leave without her agreeing to his offer.

She'd been on the edge yesterday. Today, he'd do whatever was necessary to tip her over.

ON FLOOR TWELVE, Mercy had a total of five stops. Three dogs, two hotel-supplied goldfish. Spiffed up in her hotel uniform with her kitty tie and ponytail holder she pulled her cart along, trying to remember if Jacob and Alexis were going to stay the night, or if it was Oliver and Grace.

At twelve-twenty, she knocked on the door. "Pet-Quarters." As she waited, she held on to the fish food in her pocket. She'd brought a new, clean dog bed for Corkie, the beautiful cocker spaniel mix who was currently being bathed with a lavender dog shampoo Mercy liked quite a bit. She knocked again, made one more shout out that she was from PetQuarters, then used her pass key to enter the room.

Mostly, the guests weren't there at two in the afternoon. She wasn't sure why, but she found more guests in from noon to one than two to three, so that's when she, or one of the other permanent staff, made house calls.

Inside the room, which was a junior suite, she went first to the fishbowl. She'd actually come up with the idea—loaning fish to guests who might like some company. Mr. Evans had been charmed by the idea and said he'd gotten the fish as a companion for Corkie.

He'd chosen a gorgeous Siamese fighting fish, brilliant blue with a double tail. The fish had been given the unimaginative name Blue, but he'd ignored the indignity and become one of the most sought-after of the loaners.

She tapped the side of the bowl, causing Blue to investigate. Before she got to feeding him his delicious mix of betta pellets and frozen bloodworms, she figured she'd get Corkie's bedding taken care of.

Corkie, like most of the pets who spent their nights with their parents, slept in the bedroom. Mercy got the new bed from her cart and brought it close so she could sniff. They got the beds from a small company in New Jersey who stuffed them with Poly-Fil and cedar chips, which the dogs seemed to love. This one was light green and smelled like comfort.

She got two new packs of their homemade food along with several treats to put on Corkie's place mat.

The bedroom door was closed, so just to be sure she knocked, loudly. "PetQuarters." After a full minute with no response, she opened the door, calling out once more.

It was dark, the drapes drawn. Mercy stepped inside and turned on the light.

There was Corkie's food bowl, empty, and there was Mr. Evans, completely and utterly naked, tied to the bed, gagged and, in a sight that would haunt her for years to come, erect.

Mercy froze. She'd heard stories about things like this, but she'd never actually seen it. Mr. Evans had come to PetQuarters three days ago, where he'd picked out Blue and introduced her to Corkie. He was a magazine publisher or editor, something like that, and she remembered quite clearly seeing the wedding band on his finger.

He'd seemed nice. Normal. Frankly, he'd seemed like he'd be much smaller.

He made a sound and she realized she'd been staring. With a blush that could have started forest fires, she turned off the light and backed out of the bedroom.

Murmuring "Oh, God" over and over she stood by the door, her hands filled with dog accessories, her mind screaming at what she'd just seen.

Aside from the incredibly naked man, there had been other…things. Things from the sex chest. Things she didn't think a guy would use, at least not by himself.

But he'd been tied up. He couldn't have done that on his own, right? Someone had to have been there to gag him. To wrap the rope around his ankles. Or…someone was still there. A woman. Maybe his wife? Or maybe it was a man!

She should leave. Now. Go hit herself on the head with something heavy so she'd forget what she'd seen. Forever.

But what if he was in trouble? What if he'd been hurt? If she ran, and he died, she'd feel horrible. Wouldn't she? Yes. Yes, she would. That would be a terrible thing.

It wasn't as if she hadn't seen a naked guy before. Usually they were younger and in a lot better shape, but it wasn't the worst thing she'd ever witnessed.

She'd just go back in, untie the man and leave. The end. No big deal. No need for her face to flame or her hand to shake as she turned the bedroom doorknob.

The light went on, proving to her that no matter how desperate and justified the wish was, there were no magic elves. It was just her and Mr. Naked Erection Man.

She cleared her throat as she put down the dog supplies on one of the cushy chairs. Then, telling herself there was no need to freak out, she approached the bed. She'd undo the gag first. That way, he could tell her to get out. Or to call 911.

Her steps felt leaden as she got closer to the bed. Jesus, she looked at it. Him. It. Her gaze skirted away to something safe. The wall. The nice pastel wall.

She could still see Naked Man, but only in her peripheral vision, which was still too much. But she made it to the head of the bed and saw that the gag had been tied pretty tightly.

Through squinted eyes, she located the knot. She had to lean over to get to it, and crap, crap, she looked at *it* again. She shut her eyes tight, but then she lost where the knot was.

Opening her eyes just a bit, she found the knot again. Her hands were shaking so it was hard to untie the damn thing, but she held her breath and went for it. Finally, the knot gave and she pulled the gag out of Mr. Evans's mouth.

"Thank God," he said, right before he coughed.

"Are you hurt?" she asked, her voice so high she sounded like a mouse.

"No. I'm not hurt at all."

Although the words should have reassured her, they had the exact opposite effect. Against her will, Mercy looked at Mr. Evans. His smile was so wrong it made her skin crawl.

"The only thing wrong with me is that I'm lonely."

"You're…"

"Why don't you stay? I promise, I'll make it worth your while."

"I— Are you kidding?"

"I never kid when I'm this horny, beautiful."

Mercy took a step back, then another. Until her back hit the bedroom door. Two seconds later, she was on the other side, Mr. Married Naked Pervert still calling out to her to stay.

She grabbed her cart and got the hell out of there, still

freaked, still blushing, still mortified. It wasn't until she was halfway to the elevator that she remembered.

This time, she didn't knock. She didn't call out, or even bring the cart in. She ran straight to the fishbowl, fed Blue and ran out of there.

She was still shaking when she got back to PetQuarters, where she went into her office, closed the door and renewed her pledge to keep the hell away from humans, especially the males.

5

THE FIRST SOUND Will heard when he entered the main room at PetQuarters wasn't dogs barking or playing, it was people laughing. A whole group of them, standing near the dog suites. It was so raucous even the pets were staring.

He walked toward them slowly, not wanting to break things up. As he rounded the big-dog pen, he saw that Mercy was at the center of the hilarity, only she wasn't laughing. Her smile was tight, her body language stressed.

His hackles rose as he watched. Couldn't they see she didn't find the situation funny? That she wanted to run?

Moving carefully, he got close enough to hear what was going on. At least, most of it.

"I met him," one of the team said. He was a tall young man with emo hair and a slacker's insolence. "He's Joe Suburb. Damn, can you imagine what his wife has to put up with?"

That got another laugh.

One of the girls, someone he'd never seen before, shivered dramatically. "I totally would have hurled. I mean, please. We do *not* get paid enough to put up with that shit."

"So what did you do?"

Mercy took a deep breath, then went back to the fake smile. "I called security."

"Who?" This by the tall girl, Gilly. "Was it Frank? Please tell me it was Frank."

"I don't know," Mercy said. "I didn't care, as long as I didn't have to go back into that room."

So something had happened in a guest room. To Mercy. Will had to take his own deep breath. His reaction was strong and odd. Mercy was clearly safe, she didn't look hurt. But still, it had to have been something dramatic.

"Can you imagine Frank walking into that bedroom?" Gilly said. "Seeing that perv with his hard-on sticking up?"

Everyone cracked up since clearly Frank wasn't the type to find a guy in that condition funny. Everyone but Mercy.

She'd walked into a room where some guy had been naked. Will felt hot all over and curling his hands into fists wasn't cutting it. He wanted to know who this guy was, and then he wanted to go teach him a lesson he wouldn't forget.

Instead, he breathed slowly and concentrated on Mercy.

"One time?" the new girl said. She was short, round, with a large smile. "My mom, who was a housekeeper at the Plaza? She told me she walked into a room? And some guy was doing a headstand, only he was naked?"

That not only brought on a new round of laughter, but the competition. He watched as four of the team stepped forward. Not that there was much room, but that didn't matter. They had stories of their own, and they would not be stopped from telling them.

Which was good. It would allow Mercy to ease out of the spotlight. Others had seen worse, right? What she'd seen was nothing.

Only he knew it wasn't nothing. For a person like Mercy, who had dark secrets, being blindsided by a sexual situation was a very big deal. Who knows what it brought up for her. And how she would withdraw as a result.

"No, wait. Listen." It was the only other guy in the group. Andrew. "I have this friend at the Four Seasons. He told me about this one couple. I swear this is true 'cause he saw it with his own two eyes. The couple, they were like young, and pretty hot. Only, they had figured out the exact place to drill a hole between their bathroom and the bathroom next to them. They even hid the hole from the maids. But they could totally see everything in the other bathroom."

"Ew," Gilly said.

"No shit." Andrew leaned farther in. "They got busted when the woman next door heard them doing it on the floor in the next room. And when security went in, they found a whole video camera thing so the two of them could watch and screw at the same time."

A chorus of groans followed. Will detoured around a big stuffed monkey so he would be just behind and a little to the left of Mercy.

As he'd expected, she noticed a presence, but seemed surprised to find out it was him. Once she saw him, he took two steps back, forcing her farther from the center of the group.

"Mr. Desmond."

"Will." He smiled.

She ducked her head. "Will," she said softly, then looked up again. "Would you like to see Buster?"

"I would."

Mercy checked, but no one was paying much attention to her. She slipped away and led Will to Buster's suite. Once Will was inside, she looked back at her team.

They were still laughing, still trying to top each other.

Will sat down on the far edge of Buster's bed, leaving Mercy plenty of room to join him. He didn't look at her though. He just said "Hey" to Buster, who was extraordinarily happy to see him.

A few moments later, blinded by licking, Will felt the bed dip. She wasn't exactly close, but it was still a bold move, considering.

"He's such a sweet boy," she said.

"Yeah. I think I picked a winner."

"Here's something though. As much fun as it is to be slathered with doggy spit, it's not a great idea."

He glanced across the little bed. Mercy met his gaze for just a few seconds. "What do you mean?"

"Well, if you're serious about training Buster, you need to start now, teaching him who's boss."

"The licking's not that bad."

"It's not just licking. Buster needs someone to look up to. He's a dog and he's more comfortable if he has someone he can count on. By laughing and giving him affection when he's like this, all excited, he learns that jumping all over you and licking your face is a good thing to do."

"When is giving him affection good?"

"After he's done something to deserve it. Like sitting or fetching or just being still for a moment."

"Isn't he a little young for that?"

She shook her head and gave him another quick glance. "He's old enough."

Will put Buster on the floor. "Sit," he said.

Buster jumped up on his leg.

"Sit!"

Buster jumped some more.

Mercy got up and corrected Buster with a click of her fingers and a touch. Like magic, Buster backed down, flopped on the floor and waved his paws in the air. "See, he's submissive. You can reward him with a pat now. Let him know he's a very good boy."

Will hesitated for a minute, then crouched down next to Buster and proceeded to make an utter fool of himself. He tugged on the other end of the stuffed taco, tickled the dog's tummy, had his fingers nibbled as well as his eight-hundred-dollar shoes. He didn't look at Mercy, not even once. His entire focus was on Buster, who played his part to perfection.

Finally, he heard it. Mercy's laughter. He grinned up at her, and yep, she was smiling. Her posture had changed for the better. "I think he's winning."

She nodded. "Yep."

"Is all this kosher? Playing with him like this?"

She perched on the edge of the bed. From his position on the floor, he saw the bed was just a regular twin mattress built on a storage box. It was smart. He wasn't sure what was in storage, but he imagined toys and maybe food, and he wouldn't doubt a change of mattress pads to quickly take care of accidents.

"Playing with Buster is the best thing of all. He's already quite socialized, but he could use all the human interaction he can get."

At the mention of his name, Buster went straight to Mercy's sneakers to attack her laces. Mercy deflected the attack with a quick pickup. She held him on her lap, where she gave him gentle corrections as he nipped. "The chewing is completely normal. He'll keep it up until he's about a year old, but he needs to know what's okay to chew and what's not." She reached into her coat pocket and pulled out a small plastic bone. The moment Buster saw it, he forgot about everything and attacked the bone.

"How did you learn this stuff?" Will asked. He stayed on the floor, but made himself more comfortable.

"I read books, watched videos. Working at the shelter helped. I saw firsthand how people can screw up a dog. It's really not complicated to give a dog a long, happy life. But people are…"

"Stupid?" he offered.

She laughed. "Pretty much."

Will let the conversation slide as he watched her play with the dog. There was no denying she had a gift with the little guy. He was on the bed now, on his back, wiggling and happy. While Mercy wasn't wiggling, she'd left the disturbing matter of the naked guy behind her, at least for now. "I always wanted a dog when I was a kid. My folks were against it. Too much work, too much money."

"I know. I've never had my own dog."

"You're kidding."

She shook her head. "I would sometimes go to local dog parks. Mostly, nobody minded if I played with the puppies. That was nice."

"I'd be willing to bet those owners were glad to have someone else run around with their pets. I know a lot of people who expect dogs to amuse themselves."

"Oh, yeah. That happens all the time. That's one of the reasons I'm trying to expand our day care business. Instead of leaving their dogs in their apartments all day, they can come here to play. It's so much better for the animals, and then when their parents are home with them, everyone's happier."

As the minutes ticked on, Will listened to Mercy explain all the ways the dogs in her care thrived. She played with Buster the whole time, gently showing him how to behave.

He thought again about how attractive she was. His type had always been tall, dark women with smoky eyes who had no desire to get involved. Not that he was against blondes, but they'd never captured his imagination. Not until Mercy.

He wondered how her long, straight hair would look on a pillow, how it would feel brushing his thighs. Would she be blonde everywhere?

She laughed, which made him smile. He knew she didn't do that often, especially with people, and that became a new goal. Find out everything about the diamond dog collar, and make Mercy laugh.

Had her sense of humor been knocked out of her by whatever horrors were in her past? A surge of anger surprised him as he thought again about the naked guy. Will felt sure that what Mercy needed was a whole lot of nurturing when it came to naked men. Like the puppies she watched over, she deserved the kind of gentle care that would make her feel safe. Let her play.

He'd like to think he could do that for her. Not that he considered himself a Casanova, but he did know a great deal about people, about what was underneath.

Unlike Mercy, his early life had been all about family. Not in the *Leave it to Beaver* sense, but still— family. His had been a tight-knit group. He had a brother and a sister, although his brother was dead four years now. Will hadn't spoken to his sister since his mother had died, and that was, what, eight years ago? As for his father, well, he'd been killed in a robbery when Will had been twelve.

After his father's death, his uncles, cousins and grandparents had swooped up the family in caring but smothering arms. He'd never really understood why his mother had put up with it. The family would have been fine left on their own. Although it had been the family who made sure Will got into Harvard. He'd gotten a scholarship, too, but they'd supplied him with enough money that he hadn't had to work during the school year.

He couldn't deny that growing up he'd loved the big brood. But once he realized who they really were and what they expected from him, he'd run as far as he could.

"Will?"

"Sorry, did you ask me something? I got lost watching you two."

"I have to get back to work. The little guys need to go to the park."

"Ah, I see. Will Buster be going?"

She nodded.

"Would it disturb things if I went, too?"

"Are you sure? We try and take the whole bunch of them at once. There are eight, split between us. That's a lot of dogs."

He stood up. "I think I can handle it."

"We'll be gone for an hour, at least."

"Let's rock."

She grinned as she handed him Buster. "Okay, don't say I didn't warn you."

MERCY BIT BACK a laugh as Will got tangled in leashes. Again. She'd tried to warn him that walking the dogs, even the tiny ones, wasn't as easy as it looked, but he'd blown off her advice. Now, he had four dogs, each of them trying to go in a different direction and looping his legs in the process.

Her dogs, on the other hand, were being remarkably well-behaved, considering they had so much to distract them.

It didn't help that they were on a particularly popular section of Madison Avenue, and that the pedestrians, normally well-mannered and used to dog walkers, were being very unsympathetic toward Will's dilemma.

"All right. That's enough." Will untangled his legs and got everyone heading in the right direction. "Now, do you want to go to the park or not?"

"That's right," she said. "Logic gets them every time."

He gave her a look that was meant to be scathing, but it just made her laugh.

"Will, you have to be the top dog. Stop being so scared."

"Scared?" He seemed terribly affronted. "They're all snack size."

"Doesn't matter." She walked ahead with her charges, all four of them, trotting in a neat row, two on either side of her. She turned her head back. "They need to respect you as the pack leader. Get calm, don't get mad."

He followed, but his group, once more, scrambled all over the place. Buster, naturally, was the worst of them, jumping up on Will's leg to get his attention.

Mercy walked on. Will would figure it out. He was good at calming things down. That, she'd learned from personal experience. Although he'd played his hand subtly, she wasn't so naive that she hadn't caught on. Back at PetQuarters, he'd eased her away from the team and distracted her with adorableness. She'd given herself over to the ploy willingly, and to her surprise it had worked. Her stomach was no longer in knots and the tension in her shoulders had eased.

It had been an exceptionally kind thing to do. She'd never imagined distraction alone could work so well. All her buttons had been pushed by that naked asshole, and she'd been heading right for a crash, but now, when she thought about facing the idiotic pervert, she felt no guilt, no blame. Only disgust and pity.

Not that she ever wanted anything like that to happen again. It had been horrible. But she was here, now, on this warm afternoon, heading to play at the park. It was one of her favorite parts of the job, and having Will as a companion…? Well, that was something.

Gilly, the snake, had made sure Will was her only companion. Faking, and faking so obviously it was ridiculous, an errand emergency, Gilly had asked Will if he would mind terribly taking the little puppies solo.

The moment he'd agreed, Gilly had headed straight for the grooming room, her "emergency" magically forgotten.

But he'd been a good sport about the whole thing, and besides, it gave him a chance to work with Buster. It was a pity he wasn't going to keep the dog. The two of them made a great pair.

"Uh, Mercy?"

She stopped just before the corner and turned. She laughed again, really amused at just how screwed up four leashes could get. This time, he required assistance. She threaded leashes through his arms and legs. Instead of giving him back his dogs, she traded, letting him take the calmer dogs down the last block.

The dogs got a little unruly when they smelled what was ahead, and they all walked a little faster. It was a relief to everyone when they entered the dog park. A few moments later, all the leashes were taken off the puppies and the whole gang charged into the fray.

"That was good," she said. "For a first time."

"Don't patronize me, Ms. Jones. I'm very aware I screwed the pooch. Pardon the pun."

"There is no pardon for that." She led him to the benches by the big tree. Although there were about a half-dozen dogs and several other owners, there was still room for them in the shade. Once they sat, they just watched the dogs.

"Buster's happy."

"He is. He likes group play. I hope your nephew has somewhere to take him."

"I haven't checked it out, but I will. It'll be good for both of them."

She nodded. "It's a pity you can't keep Buster for your own."

"I travel too much. It wouldn't be fair."

"No, that's wise. It takes time to make a happy dog."

Will gave her a smile before he went back to watching. "I was right. This is turning out to be a great vacation."

"How long until you go home?"

"I don't know. It depends on business, actually. I'm waiting to hear about a meeting. Personally, I hope it's not too soon."

She squeezed the leashes in her hand as she reminded herself not to take his words to heart. He was enjoying his visit. He hadn't meant that he wanted to be near her. That was just wishful thinking. And too much Gilly.

A ball hit Will in the foot. It was smaller than a tennis ball, which brought all the mini-dogs running. He threw the thing, and the whole group of them turned, some more gracefully than others, to go fetch.

Lulu was the winner of this round, and she brought the ball straight back. The pampered little thing had surprised Mercy on several occasions but none more than when they were in the park. Usually dogs like Lulu had no idea how to play with others. They were more comfortable with humans than animals, and they tended to be fearful and aggressive. Not Lulu. She was a perfect dog-park puppy. So much so that Will got up from his shaded seat and started playing a game of catch. Not just with Lulu, of course, but she retrieved the best of any of them. Buster got the ball once, and then Will was off, chasing Buster all over the place until he finally wrestled the ball free. That was the end of that game.

Will came back to the bench. He was breathing hard, but he had a big smile on his face. God, those dimples.

"So what's the deal with that diamond collar?"

"It's crazy, isn't it? Such ostentation. The dog doesn't care."

"I find it hard to believe it's the real McCoy."

"Oh, it's real, all right. And insured to the max. I asked Lulu's parents to let me put it in the hotel safe, but they wouldn't hear of it. I think they're nuts. Even if they did want to show off with the thing, she doesn't need to wear it every day. Something's bound to happen."

"What do you mean?"

"Lulu's a little ruffian. She plays hard, loves to roll around in the dirt. One of those diamonds is bound to come off, don't you think?"

He nodded. "Not to mention the whole issue of theft."

Mercy shrugged. "I know. But animal parents can be very, very peculiar."

"That isn't limited to animal parents."

She thought briefly about earlier, in Mr. Evans's room. "That's true." She debated not saying anything, but decided that wasn't fair. "Thank you, by the way."

"For what?"

"You know. All that playing with Buster. Helping me escape."

"I didn't do a thing."

"Right," she said. "But thanks, anyway."

He reached over and took her hand in his. He didn't hold it for long. Just gave her a squeeze, then let her go. But his touch reverberated, giving her a thrill not just because he'd touched her, but once again, he'd been gentle as well as personal. He hadn't bugged her with questions or felt sorry for her, or any of the normal crap.

It was a pity she hadn't known someone like him years ago. It would have helped. A lot. "You know, I'm going to be staying late tonight. If you wanted to have some private lessons, I think we could do that."

He turned to her. Smiled. Gave her one little nod, and it was done.

6

_____

AFTER HE DISABLED the alarm, Will unlocked the door to find a pile of mail waiting for him. He hadn't been home in several days, and while most of his mail went to the office, he still had his personal stuff to attend to.

He flipped on the light, comforted to see everything as he'd left it. He'd only lived in SoHo for two years, and it had taken his designer most of that time to get the co-op right. One of his hobbies was collecting modern art, so the lighting and all the decor focused on the walls. On his paintings.

His gaze went naturally to the big Hockney. It always made him feel calmer to look into the blue swimming pool, to see the neat white structures and all that color. But he didn't have time to waste. It was five, and he was meeting Mercy at PetQuarters at seven-thirty.

After gathering the mail he went to his small kitchen, all gleaming stainless steel and glass, and dialed Hush. It took him just a few minutes to handle his business. He got a bottle of German lager from his fridge, and sat down to go through his real life.

Even as he sorted his bills from his solicitations and invitations, the quiet pressed down on him. He should have turned on some music, but now it felt foolish. He wasn't going to be there long enough for it to matter.

He looked forward to tonight. Spending time with Mercy was an unexpected treat. Maybe he just didn't get out enough. When he did, it was invariably something that somehow was good for business. Even his season tickets to the Met were more for show than for enjoyment. He rarely cared for opera, but he went anyway. Just like he showed up at fund-raisers for all the right causes, and donated just enough to be noticed.

When was the last time he was at a park? Oh, yeah. Shakespeare. That was at least a great play. He'd paid five hundred bucks for him and his date to sit on a blanket and eat cold chicken, but the money had gone to AmFar, so at least on that occasion, everyone won. Today had been a lot more fun, though.

He looked back into the living room and tried to imagine Buster there. Jesus. His furniture had cost a fortune. The carpet alone cost more than he'd earned at his first legit job. No. His life wouldn't mix with a dog. He barely did anything here but sleep these days. It wasn't an accident that there was no actual food in his fridge. Beer, yes. Wine. Champagne. And of course, olives, onions. The basics. If he needed to eat he ordered from one of the hundreds of nearby restaurants. Usually Chinese from down the street.

He had a maid, of course, who was bonded within an inch of her life, but she did a good job and she understood how to care for fine art. It was a showplace, all right. Someday he'd entertain here. Have dinner parties or screenings. But for now, it was a good investment.

He took care of his bills, shredded sensitive papers,

tossed a bunch of crap, including a letter from his sister, and by the time he'd finished, his beer was gone, his appetite was revived and it was time to go.

He did a quick walk-through of the whole place, just in case, then reset the alarm and locked the door. One hour, ten minutes.

"THAT WAS WEIRD."

Mercy looked over at Gilly, who was filling food bowls. "Do you notice that she never even bothers to come get Pumpkin anymore? I swear she just comes by to complain."

"She didn't even want to pick Pumpkin up. Bitch," Gilly said.

"Maybe I can convince her that she'd be better off without a dog."

"Maybe. Now, are you going to tell me about the park, or am I going to have to torture you?"

Mercy felt her cheeks flame up. "It was fine."

"That tells me exactly nothing." Gilly poured a ton of food into Rio's bowl. The dog ate an incredible amount, but then he was the size of a Buick.

"He wasn't very good on the walk. Either way. But he was a good sport about it."

"Yeah, yeah. Dogs, walk, yippee. That's not what I need to hear."

"That's all you're going to get because nothing else happened."

Gilly put her hands on her hips. "Mercy, I swear to God if you blow this… Will Desmond is so into you it's not even funny. And who knows when he's going back to Idaho."

"Kansas."

"Whatever. Give yourself a break, girl. You're not a nun. You're young, healthy and damn it, a vibrator can only do so much."

"Gilly!"

"What? I'm just sayin'. He's gorgeous. He wants you. He's here. What do you want, an engraved invitation?"

"It's not that simple."

"But it is." Gilly's voice had gone soft. "It's boy meets girl, the oldest story in the world. You like him, he likes you. Getting close is a good thing. A healing thing. I promise you'll be so…so glad you did."

"You promise, huh?"

"I do. You know what Eleanor Roosevelt said?"

Mercy laughed. "Eleanor Roosevelt?"

"Don't mock. It's good stuff. She said, 'You must do the thing you can't do.'" Her face scrunched up. "There's more, or maybe it's the thing you can do. I forget. But it's important for you to step out of your comfort zone. If he turns out to be a dog? So what? You're used to dogs. Besides, he's gonna be history before you know it. You get to choose whether you have a memory that will carry you through, or a regret that will haunt you."

"When did you become Ms. Philosophy?"

"Shut up. You know I'm right."

Mercy went back to food preparation, but Gilly's advice played too damn loudly in her brain. She'd had such a bad experience this morning. It made perfect sense to retreat. To let herself get over it in her own way. On the other hand, her own way hadn't been very successful, had it? What if the perfect antidote to seeing horrible naked stranger was to be with gorgeous naked friend?

He was a friend, wasn't he? Okay, maybe not a BFF, but they were definitely not strangers.

She didn't have to decide right this second. She'd wait 'til he got here. See how the training went. See how she felt. He might not even want her like that. One thing for sure. No way she was making the first move.

MAYBE SHE SHOULD make the first move.

"Good boy!" Will said, as he crouched down low to give Buster a treat. "You're the best boy. What a champion. Look, all the other dogs want to be near you. They want to *be* you. You're going to be the damn poster dog of obedience in no time, aren't you?"

Mercy grinned. She'd thought Will was cute before, but he'd just moved up three levels. And he'd only been at PetQuarters half an hour.

"What's next?"

"Let's keep working on 'sit.'"

"But he just—"

"One time isn't a conditioned response. Sorry."

He stood up. "Don't you listen to her, Buster. You and I both know you're the best sitter in the whole world." He arched his brow at Mercy, then walked a few feet from the dog. "Come, Buster. Come."

Buster, who knew a treat machine when he met one, ran full tilt, his ears flapping away.

"Sit," Will said, using just the right mix of gentle and assertive.

Buster instantly rolled onto his back and barked.

Will sighed. "It's close."

"It is. Now help him make it perfect."

He crouched down again, and then the night buzzer rang, scaring them all, especially Buster, who flipped over and crawled between Will's legs.

"Work with him," she said. "I'll be right back." The bell had surprised her because they weren't really expecting any new pets tonight. Eddy and Andrew were the designated sitters, but she'd let them go out to dinner. Well, *forced* them was more like it. And she didn't doubt for a moment they knew why. But she didn't care. She'd made up her mind. She was going to go for it with Will. Tonight. Maybe.

She went into the reception area and found a room service waiter she didn't know standing in the little lobby. "Can I help you?"

"Dinner for Mr. Desmond and guest?"

"Oh." He'd ordered dinner? From room service? Holy— She'd planned on a PowerBar and an apple. "Come on in."

The nice waiter followed her into PetQuarters, where he didn't seem to think it was at all odd to find Mr. Desmond on the floor with a puppy on his tummy.

"Shall I set up here, sir?"

"Ask the lady," he said, then went right back to playing with Buster.

She thought about it for a second, then led the waiter to her office. It wasn't huge, and there were a lot of plates and silver and glasses, but in the end, it was perfect. Eddy and Andrew would be at a safe distance while she and Will ate.

When she went back to the main room, Will was standing and Buster was in his suite munching on a bone.

Will signed for the meal, waited for the waiter to leave, then took her hand in his. "I hope it's okay. I figured since you're here because of me, the least I could do—"

"It's nice," she said, blushing yet again. "Thank you."

"Come on. Let's eat before it gets cold."

He led her all the way to her office, never letting go of her hand. It wasn't half-bad. In fact, the feel of his warm hand was pretty wonderful.

"I had no idea if you were a vegetarian or a carnivore or what, so I ordered a few different things." He lifted up the silver domes over three plates. The first was a steak, baked potato and some wonderful-looking broccoli. The second had a salmon filet, fancy green beans and even fancier potatoes in a little pot. The third was pasta. A gorgeous huge bowl of fettuccini alfredo with a side salad.

"Your pick," he said.

"How can I chose? They all look incredible."

"Then have all three."

She laughed. "There's no way."

"Why not? We'll split them all. Eat what we want, laugh at the rest."

Her gaze moved from the stunning food to the even more stunning man. "You're crazy."

"Naw. I'm just on vacation." He pointed to three smaller dishes, each one still covered. "I'm not even going to tell you how incredible the desserts are, but trust me. Leave room."

She nodded. Wished she could think of something to say. Anything. Instead, she nodded again.

Will, in yet another attempt to fluster her, came around the desk and held her chair for her. It was amazing. And a little awkward. But then she had her napkin on her lap, he'd poured them each some wine and he was ready to eat.

"Enjoy," he said.

"Wow," she said back.

He chuckled, and cut himself a nice bite of steak. That was all the permission she needed, and she dug right in. The pasta made her swoon, and soon she was tasting everything. There wasn't a single thing that wasn't incredible.

He wasn't being particularly shy about eating, either. They didn't talk that much—too much chewing—but it was fine. Surprisingly comfortable. It helped that he groaned with pleasure with most of his bites, and smiled at her as if they were two kids in a candy store.

Even the wine was good. She wasn't much of a connoisseur. In fact, she found most wines to be too…something. Not exactly bitter, but not sweet, either. This one was just right. It didn't burn at all when it went down.

"I still think Buster knows what 'sit' means," he said, after they'd both gotten over their initial panic. "He's smart as a whip."

"I'm sure he is," she said. "Brilliant."

"Don't laugh. I saw he was smart from the first day."

"I'm not laughing. Honestly. Just know that even the smartest dogs need a lot of repetition and practice. Don't get discouraged if it takes longer than ten minutes to teach him the next thing."

"Fine. But you'll see. He's going to knock your socks off."

She took another forkful of salmon. "I'm counting on it."

He held up his glass of wine. "To Buster, the brilliant."

She lifted her glass and tapped it against his. "And to his remarkable Uncle Will."

They both drank, and when she put her glass down, Will was staring at her. He'd lost his silly grin, and it seemed he wasn't very hungry anymore, as he'd put his fork down.

She got self-conscious, of course, but it wasn't all that bad. The dinner glow was still with her, but even that couldn't compete with the pleasure she'd gotten from their little training session.

"You're a beautiful woman," he said.

"No," she said. "I'm not really."

"Yes, you are. There's a light inside you that just shines."

"That's just my stupid blush. I can't help it. I've always been this way."

His hand moved forward until he touched hers. "It's way more than that, Mercy. I've enjoyed this so much. The park was a real treat, and tonight…? Well, even if Buster hadn't learned how to sit the moment the word was spoken, it would have been great."

She wished like crazy that she knew what to do. There must be something cool or suave or—please—not horrible that she could say. Something that would let him know that she was…she was… "Yeah," she whispered.

The man pulled out his dimples. It wasn't fair, but then, what part of life was? His grin made him look young and sweet and she wanted to kiss him.

That notion alone made her hand jerk back. Why had she thought she could be a normal girl? She was broken, and a beautiful man who loved dogs and ordered three dinners wasn't going to fix her. "You said something about dessert?"

"Dessert! Yes. I did. You've had enough of the dinner part?"

She nodded. "It was all delicious."

"Yeah. That Amuse Bouche sure knows how to sling some hash."

"I've never—"

"Really?"

"Nah. It's kind of frowned upon. You know, employees doing hotel stuff."

"That doesn't seem fair."

"It's okay. I liked it this way."

"No candles. No hovering waiters."

"Yeah. I never have liked candles."

Will stood up and stacked their dinner plates. Then he put the three small plates with their nice little domes in the center of her desk. Good thing she hardly ever used the thing. Of course, from now until forever, she'd walk in this room and see Will and all the food, and she hoped beyond hope that Gilly was right and that the memory would be wonderful.

"First," he said. "I give you…chocolate." He whisked the dome off the plate to reveal the most unbelievable concoction. It was tall and dark but with some kind of creamy sauce and a lattice thingy made from what looked like caramel.

"Oh, man. I really like chocolate."

"Wait. There's more." With a dramatic wave of his hand, he touched the second dome, then stopped. "May I introduce you to—" he sprung the lid "—lavender crème brûlée."

It looked spectacular. Crunchy all over the top, a little tiny sparkly flower on one side. "I love crème brûlée."

"Ah. So creamy custard trumps chocolate."

"Not by much."

"And for our last contestant, I present…" He lifted the last dome and there was the most beautiful, most delicate and perfect dessert in the world.

"Raspberry tart with almond meringue and toasted pistachios."

"Will? I might have to eat all of these."

"I see."

She looked him right in the eyes. "By myself."

"But—"

"No. You're right. It's completely selfish. Awful, really. I mean, you bought the dinner. You picked the desserts out, so you must like each one very much. And you're so nice, not to mention a guest. But I don't think it matters."

He picked up her dessert fork and handed it to her. "I will be delighted and enchanted to sit back and watch."

"Will?"

"Yes?"

"I'm kidding."

The way his face changed. His head tilted to the right and he looked as if she'd done a magic trick, plucked roses out of thin air.

"I know," she said. "Most people think I had my sense of humor surgically removed."

"No, no. It's just… You surprised me. I don't get surprised often."

She lifted her fork. "I have to try that tart."

"Please."

The meringue crumbled as she dipped in, but she managed to get all the different flavors on her fork. It touched her tongue with diamonds. With pearls. She moaned so loudly it sounded downright sexy.

Will laughed. Such a great sound. Honest. Full of pleasure, not mocking in any way.

"You have to try this."

He leaned over and scooped up a piece of his own. "Oh, yeah. Oh, baby. This is evil. This could start wars."

She laughed. "What a thing to say. Start wars?"

"Okay. Fistfights."

She took another bite. "That's better."

Between them, they made sure there wasn't a crumb left. He put down his fork and groaned. "I'm stuffed."

"Me, too." But her fork, it was poised over the chocolate whatsit. "Is that all you got, Desmond?"

"A dare, huh?"

She smiled.

He picked up his fork once more. "You're on."

They both dove in, and it was worth every single calorie…which had to be in the zillions.

The second bite was just as heavenly. And the third. He'd totally gotten into the spirit of things, matching her fork for fork. Finally, there was one bite left. They both dove for it at the same time, and there was a struggle. Her napkin fell off the side of the desk, and they both went for it at the same time.

Her hand touched one corner. His another. Bent over, they were inches from each other, almost touching.

She froze. Time slowed.

And then he kissed her.

7

HE TASTED LIKE CHOCOLATE.

Soft lips, gentle pressure. Mercy had been kissed before, but not like this. Not so sweetly. Was this really happening? To her?

The tip of his tongue slipped across her sensitive lower lip, urging her to relax. To open herself to him. She did, a little.

He moaned as he dipped inside, touching her teeth. She should have opened her mouth as well as parted her lips, but they were both still bent over, their hands holding the pink linen napkin. Her fork was in her other hand, her breath stolen by this amazing man.

She thought of the dessert still waiting on the desk, but her appetite had gone. For crème brûlée, at least.

Will moaned once more, then inched away. She felt the cool air of her office on her moist lips and she wanted him back. Not enough to do anything about it, though.

With the familiar sensation of her blush, she sat back in her chair, only to realize they'd both forgotten the napkin on the floor.

When she got her nerve up, she looked at Will. She expected to see disappointment, or at the very least confusion, in his eyes. But that wasn't it at all. He wanted…her.

That's what this dinner was about. And the private training sessions. And the walk to the park. Gilly had been right. The truth of it made her dizzy.

She'd been wanted before, but it hadn't been like this. Even when she'd been a willing participant, it had left her feeling empty. Used.

Maybe she would feel that way with Will, too, but somehow she doubted it.

"I don't think I have the strength to ignore the crème brûlée," Will said.

She remembered where she was. How she'd wanted that creamy delight. She still did, but she wasn't sure she had an inch of space left in her. "I'm really full."

"I know. Do you have any idea how much time I'm going to have to spend in the gym? The brûlée is only going to make things worse."

"You're right. A hundred percent right."

"It's okay. This isn't the last crème brûlée in the world," he said, as his spoon zeroed in on the crispy coating. "It would be ridiculous to eat another bite."

She picked up her spoon. "Absurd."

He broke the coating with a crackle. "I should probably go to the hotel gym right now. Get in a session on the treadmill." He scooped up a big spoonful and brought it toward his mouth. "Only a fool would eat this now." Then it was done. The spoon came out empty, and Will's eyes rolled with pleasure.

"Only a fool," she repeated, and tasted the dessert of the gods.

They didn't polish it off, but they came close. Mercy had laughed at his moaning, but she'd done some of her own. "That was the best dinner I've ever had," she confessed.

"It was right up there. Oh, I'd better call for them to pick up the dishes."

She handed him the phone as she piled plates and rescued her napkin. Once everything was back on the cart and he was finished on the phone, they left her office.

"I hate this part," he said.

"I know. You really feel how much you've eaten when you stand up."

He smiled at her. "No. I meant the leaving part."

"Oh." She thought he was going to kiss her again, but there was a bang behind her, and she spun around.

It was Andrew. He'd dropped a box of treats on the floor and now he was staring wide-eyed at her and Will.

Ever the gentleman, Will led her to the dog suites. Buster was sleeping on the bed, his head on his little paws. He looked adorable.

"Now that looks like a good idea," Will said, keeping his voice low.

"What happened to that treadmill action?"

"I can't imagine what you're referring to."

She shook her head. "Weak."

"No. Full. Stuffed. I need to recuperate before I do anything as noble as a run."

"Hey, Mercy?"

She turned to find Andrew not ten feet away. "Yeah?"

"Did you guys come out here about five, six minutes ago?"

"No. You saw when we came out. Why?"

"It's probably nothing. Probably Eddy. I thought I saw someone going into the reception area."

Mercy shook her head. "Maybe Eddy's restocking up there."

"Yeah. You're right. Sorry to bother you."

"No bother."

Andrew gave Will a guy nod, then headed for the stockroom.

"I should go," Will said, but it was hard not to notice that something about him had changed. As if Andrew's interruption had broken a spell. She studied Will's face, and yes, he was definitely distracted. Whatever connection they'd shared in her office was gone.

"Let you get some rest," he said, but almost to himself. Then he took her hands in his.

For a split second, she thought of asking him to take her to his room. The idea was banished in an instant, but the blush remained. She ignored it. "I believe I was thanking you for dinner."

"I believe you were."

"Seriously. It was the nicest surprise I've had in years."

He smiled and it was as if he'd never left. The connection was there again, a buzz kind of like when the subway train barreled by, only without the noise.

She wanted to touch his dimples, trace them with her tongue.

"This whole day has been a treat. I'm sorry it has to end. Tomorrow, I actually have some stuff to do, but I should be back around seven. Maybe we could do this again?"

"The training? Sure."

"Fair enough," he said. "Seven it shall be."

"I'll walk you out."

He looked behind her, to the dog suites. "Buster's still out like a light."

"Puppies need a lot of sleep."

"Speaking of needing sleep. You stay. I know my way out."

When he finally disappeared behind the door, Mercy closed her eyes. He still tasted like chocolate.

IT WAS JUST 7:00 a.m. when Will dove into the water. The rooftop pool was his, at least for the moment, and he intended to make the most of it, doing as many laps as he could. He needed to get rid of his sluggishness, a result of too much rich food and a bad night.

He started slowly, a nice crawl down the long lane, waiting until the fourth stroke to steal a breath. It took him a couple of laps to get into the rhythm, but once he found it, he relaxed and stopped thinking about the swimming itself.

Instead, his thoughts once again went to Mercy. It was an odd situation, one he wasn't entirely comfortable with. She was a good kid. Now that she wasn't quite as shy, he was able to see her personality. Her humor. She'd become more attractive in all kinds of ways, which helped things. Kissing her hadn't been a chore. It had been nice. Sweet. He couldn't remember the last time a kiss had been sweet.

What confused him wasn't that he found her attractive, but that he'd left her last night. He'd clearly won her over with his attention to Buster, and sealed the deal with that dinner. If he'd pressed, he knew without a doubt Mercy would have acquiesced. He'd have taken her to his room and made love. Sometime during the night, he'd have found out about her schedule. Gotten her to tell him about Lulu's owners, and more.

He was convinced that the mystery visitor to Pet-Quarters last night had been Drina. It was just like her. She'd have found some way to break into the place, whether by stealth or force. She'd once broken into a safety deposit box that wasn't her own—he'd never figured that one out.

The odd thing was that Lulu's collar hadn't been taken. Although maybe that wasn't true. Could Drina have replaced the real deal with a fake?

He'd have to find out. Five seconds with the collar and his diamond and moissanite tester and he'd know for sure. In fact, he'd better make certain Drina was still in the hotel. It would be so like her to replace the collar, then check out, leaving the poor Pumpkin and the much poorer owners of Lulu in the dust.

His arms and legs were starting to ache, but rather then get out of the pool, he turned onto his back to float and relax.

The pool area was as beautiful as the rest of the hotel. It had a clear retractable roof, which was open, letting in the abundant sunshine. The floor was tiled gray and there were chrome sconces at wide intervals on the white walls. Next to the pool was a large Jacuzzi tub, and there were white lounge chairs and round tables lined up ready for bathers. On the far wall was a bar, not staffed at the moment, but it appeared to be fully stocked.

He thought about sharing that Jacuzzi with Mercy, but no. She had to be careful not to use the public facilities.

That meant it was his room, or nothing. Not that he hadn't thought about a tryst in the back room of PetQuarters, but he wouldn't put her at risk. At least not that much risk.

Why hadn't he at least asked last night? It wasn't like him. He never let an opportunity pass him by, especially when he was after Drina.

Feeling rested, he returned to his exercise, finding his rhythm faster this time. He should have been using the pool more often. It was much more convenient than his gym, and swimming always made him calm.

It was because of the naked guy. Of course. She'd recovered so well from her encounter that he'd forgotten, only it appeared she hadn't. To have pressed her last night would have been the worst thing he could have done. She'd have withdrawn, that was a certainty, and he didn't have time to coax her back.

So his instincts were still intact. That was reassuring. He'd played the whole night perfectly. Mercy had been dazzled.

He'd do his best to keep her that way. To leave her with some good memories, at least about him. He couldn't guarantee he could protect her from Drina, but he'd try. Mercy belonged at Hush. He hoped, when it was all over, that she'd still have her job.

DRINA LOVED the humidity. It made her skin feel young again. She spent a lot of time in her garden during the summer. Most of her friends complained bitterly about the weather, but she blossomed like her petunias.

It felt good to be home, even if she couldn't stay. The hotel was fancy, the food and service were excellent, but she didn't want to be there. She shouldn't have been there. If Marius had still been alive…

She went to her bed of red roses and set to deadheading. It was familiar work. Comforting as so few things were these days.

She missed the sound of children.

There had been a time, not so long ago, when there were always children in her big, grassy yard. Someone had put in a sandbox and a swing set, she couldn't remember who. She'd had to buy two freezers, just to keep enough food on hand for the crowds. Oh, how the women had gossiped in her kitchen as they stirred pots and kneaded dough. That was life. Continuity.

None of the young ones cared so much anymore. They were too busy with their computers and their earphones and their text messages. It broke her heart.

This would be her last job. Once it was done, she would stay in this house, with its empty rooms and empty freezers. She would work in the garden until the weather grew cold, and then she would sit by the fire. Read. Please, God, she would keep her good vision. Her grandmother had gone blind at seventy. Drina would rather be dead.

She laughed at herself. Most of the time that was true, anyway, wasn't it? What was there to live for now, except for the flowers? Television bored her. Traveling held no allure, not even to see grandchildren. Why bother? They ignored her anyway.

So it was books and flowers. The occasional card game with some of the cousins. Those she could live without. They all cheated, and none of them were any good at it.

One more task. She wouldn't leave that hotel until she'd done it. Until she could watch the endgame with her own eyes.

Then, she would be ready. God could take her, and she'd be with Marius and oh, that was what she longed for.

This was no world to be a lonely old woman. No world at all.

MERCY SAT ACROSS from Janice Foster, in the general manager's office. She was ready for the meeting…well, as ready as she ever was. The numbers for pet services were at an all-time high. Just this morning, they'd checked in two midtown dogs who would be regulars. High-end regulars.

Janice walked in, looking her usual sophisticated, beautiful self. It would have been intimidating for Mercy to work downstairs. All the women at the front desk always seemed perfect. They weren't all gorgeous, either. But they cared about their presentation.

Mercy did her best to look nice, but her job was different. Although you wouldn't know it today.

Gilly had done her makeup.

What was more shocking—Mercy had let her.

She'd been flying since last night. The dinner had been so amazing, but nothing compared to the kiss. Kisses.

"How are you doing, Mercy?"

"Just fine, thanks, Ms. Foster."

Instead of sitting in her big executive chair, Janice perched on the edge of her desk. She looked at Mercy with real concern in her eyes, and that's when the flutters started in Mercy's stomach.

Something was wrong. They'd decided against the improvements.

"I heard about what happened yesterday."

"Oh," Mercy said, completely freaked. Had Andrew told someone she'd had dinner with a guest? That they'd kissed?

"Would you like to tell me what happened in Mr. Evans's room?"

Mercy closed her eyes as she breathed a sigh of relief. This wasn't about Will at all. "It was no big deal."

"On the contrary. It was a very big deal. Mr. Evans has been charged with indecent exposure and a few other choice things. I wasn't here, or I would have come to see you immediately. As it is, he'll never bother you again. If you'd like to make your own complaint, we'll make sure it's taken care of."

"No. No, that's okay. But what about Corkie?"

Janice's brows came down, then lifted. "Corkie's fine. He's on his way home. I had Eddy get the fish from the room."

"Then it's fine. It was just awkward."

"It was a crime, Mercy. I'm so terribly sorry it happened. I've made arrangements for you to talk to someone. A wonderful therapist."

"What? No. Honestly, Ms. Foster, I'd forgotten all about it."

Janice pushed her long red hair behind her shoulders, then moved from the desk to the chair right next to Mercy. "I know that I wouldn't be fine, and I certainly wouldn't forget about it. At least not so soon. It was a violation. Thank goodness nothing physical happened, but it was enough. I won't have it. Not to my people."

"I know that guests, they get kind of crazy. I've heard so many stories. Much worse than what happened to me. I promise, I'm okay."

Janice took a card from her jacket pocket and held it out. "Do me a favor. Hang on to this. Dr. Morgenstern is a wonderful person. She'd be very gentle. She won't push, and neither will I."

Mercy took the card and put it in her jacket.

"And you know my door is always open, right?"

Mercy nodded.

"You're valued here, Mercy. You're doing wonderful things at PetQuarters, and don't think it hasn't been noticed. It's in our best interest to make sure you feel happy and safe here."

Mercy laughed, but cut it off quickly as it sunk in that Janice was serious. "I do," she said. "I love working here."

"Good. Let's keep it that way."

Mercy knew an exit line when she heard one. "Thank you, Ms. Foster."

Janice stood and held out her hand. They shook, and Mercy, instead of feeling embarrassed or even blushing, felt proud. Not about Mr. Pervert Evans, but about her work.

She'd felt that way at the animal shelter, but it had taken a long time to feel confident about Hush. She was under no illusion that she was a typical employee. She figured she'd always be an outsider, but right at this minute, she felt as if she belonged.

WILL GOT BACK to Hush at seven-fifteen. Instead of heading straight to PetQuarters, he was on his way to his room. He needed a shower. A drink.

Today had been tiring, but good. He'd found out a lot about George and Ivy Morris, Lulu's owners. They had money, all right. Enough to buy and sell Hush. Lulu was their only child, it seemed. The diamond collar was nothing compared to what that dog would inherit.

People were insane. That's all. A damn dog?

Actually, he would be the first to admit that Buster was great. If there was any way he could keep the little guy, he would. That didn't mean he'd leave him a fortune.

He would, however, make sure he was taken care of. Loved. He hadn't figured out how, not yet, but wouldn't it be something if Buster ended up with Mercy?

Man, that would be one lucky dog.

The elevator ride was achingly slow. He stretched his neck as he thought about what he needed to do tonight. Transfer his notes into his computer. Find out if the Morrises had any other insurance companies on the books.

His friend Ricky had only found one, but there'd been something wrong with the policy. That's what had taken Will so long. He'd been in Jersey all day, reading the damn thing. Twice. Nothing jumped out at him as being crooked, but still, he couldn't shake the feeling.

Maybe after he'd relaxed with Mercy, it would come to him.

He smiled as the elevator stopped on the ninth floor.

He stepped farther back to make room for a party of four heading to the roof. They were young, beautiful, wealthy. The world was at their disposal.

He wondered how many closet skeletons per person there were in this cab? Despite looks and ready cash, no one truly had it perfect. In his experience, those with the most cash had the most to hide. Screwed-up families, hidden and not-so-hidden motivations from everyone from the butler to the boyfriend.

At least with a girl like Mercy, you knew what you were getting. She was nice in a way that didn't just feel true, but was true. She'd been hurt, and it showed, but damn, it was honest.

He thought about the way she'd felt in his arms. That last kiss had been something. She was strong, he could feel that. Strong inside and out. He hoped someday that she would see her inner strength. That it would help her find her own happiness.

Finally, he got to his floor. He stepped out, his jacket over his arm, his tie loosened, his top button undone. He felt as if he was wearing half of Manhattan.

All his discomfort disappeared as he turned down the hall.

Mercy.

She was standing by his door, looking sweet and scared and hopeful. He smiled, and the leash slid from her hand.

Buster came barreling down the carpet, barking and wagging all over the place.

Will crouched and the puppy bounded into his arms. When he stood up, Mercy was still there. Waiting.

8

MERCY'S STOMACH fluttered as Will stood. Even from six doors down the hall, she could see how pleased he was at her surprise. Or should she say it fluttered more. Her stomach had been in this tumultuous state since she'd made up her mind to do this.

On one level, it made no sense whatsoever. She had no business stepping into Will's room, except, perhaps, to bring supplies for Buster, but even that didn't wash because Buster was a full-timer at PetQuarters. That's not why she'd come, though. She'd come because…

She wasn't sure. Yes, she liked Will. More than she had anyone. And sure, there was all that stuff Gilly had said. He wasn't here but for a while; therefore, how much trouble could she get into, and all that. But neither of those reasons was the real reason.

In her heart of hearts, she knew she'd come because she was tired of being a victim. Tired of being scared of her own shadow. Tired of hiding.

In some weird way, the incident with the naked guy had changed something inside her. Not just the shock of it, but the way she'd been able to get over it. Talking to Janice Foster had made that very clear.

Mercy didn't need to go see any therapist. She'd

seen a naked, pathetic man who'd propositioned her. She hadn't been hurt, she hadn't been permanently damaged, she'd walked away. Even though it had been upsetting, it hadn't been her fault, and with Will's help, she'd been able to put the whole thing in perspective.

And perspective is what had brought her here. To this suite.

She was a healthy young woman who hadn't let herself relax with a man in years, if ever. She felt remarkably relaxed with Will. They'd clicked. There was heat between them. For once in her life, she was going to see it through. Not run, not hide, not make excuses.

Now, if only she could get her stomach to settle, this might turn out to be one of the best memories she'd ever have.

"You're the best thing I've seen all day," Will said.

"And you're the best thing Buster's seen."

Will grinned at the puppy, who was beside himself with joy, licking, wagging, making tiny little yipping noises. "He does seem pretty excited."

Despite the crazed dog in his arms, Will managed to get his card key out and swipe it. Mercy pushed the door open, and then the three of them entered a world of luxury.

She'd been in the suites before, as a lot of the wealthiest guests liked to check in with pets, but this was different. She wasn't going to do her job, then dash away. If things went well, she wouldn't leave until much, much later.

"You think it's okay to let him run around?"

"Sure. If he has an accident, we'll just clean it right up. But he had a long walk just before we rode up."

Will put Buster down and his puppy instincts took

over. There was so much to sniff. It was almost as good as the park.

Will walked her farther into the living room. After tossing his jacket on the back of the couch, he turned to her. "This is a wonderful surprise," he said. "But here's the thing. I need a drink and a shower or I won't be fit to be near you."

For a second there, her heart had pounded hard, but no, things were still fine. "Sure. I'll just watch Buster."

His head dipped and his eyes seemed darker. "The shower's big enough for two."

She blushed ferociously and nearly bolted for the door. "That's okay. I should stay out here."

"Oh," he said, and she could hear the disappointment in his voice.

She took a deep breath and faced him, even with her flaming cheeks. "I thought I could help you with Buster," she said, her voice a little too high. "And then we could…"

"See where the evening leads us?"

"Yes," she said, relieved as could be that he understood.

"Great idea. I'll go then. Get cleaned up. I won't be long."

"Take your time," she said. "I'm off work, so no one's expecting me."

He touched her cheek with the side of his hand. "I'm very glad you're here," he said. "No pressure. No worries. It's all good."

She almost closed her eyes. Let her cheek rest against his hand. But she couldn't quite get there.

He nodded, then headed for the bedroom.

The second the door was closed behind him, she collapsed on the couch. It was still hard to believe that she was here, that she had taken the bull by the horns, so to speak. Gilly was going to freak.

Buster came by, sniffed her shoes, then darted off to investigate the coffee table. God, this suite was so beautiful. She'd never just sat down before. Not like a real person. A guest. It felt totally different. As if she would suddenly have a taste for caviar.

Even an unsophisticated hick like her knew that the artwork was good. Museum good. And she wouldn't find the material on the couch cushions at any discount stores.

She'd been at Hush for over a year, but this was the first time she truly got it. This was fantasyland. A place where anything was possible.

WILL LET THE COOL WATER lower his temperature and his expectations. The moment he'd seen Mercy standing by his door, it had hit him like a ton of bricks how much he wanted her. Just picturing her in that big bed made him hard. But he didn't want his dick to take over here. She was a nice kid. Someone who deserved all the happiness she could get, and he needed to make damn sure she was in this for the right reasons.

There was nothing wrong with enjoying each other. God knows, there wasn't enough of that in his life. Or hers, as far as he could tell. But it was what it was. Nothing more.

He'd be gone as soon as the business with Drina was over. Mercy knew that he'd be leaving, but before he did anything she'd regret, he needed to make sure she understood.

As for him? He'd miss Mercy. Too bad he'd met her under these circumstances. Another time, another place, and he'd have pursued her. Not for anything serious, but she was someone he'd have liked to have as a friend. Especially a friend with benefits.

That was impossible. The only reason he was here was to stop Drina. Everything else was secondary, including Mercy. It was just a shame, that's all.

That she'd come here tonight was a win in all kinds of ways. He just needed to be careful and not let himself get all sentimental.

Mercy, in addition to all her great qualities, had a pass card that could get him into any room in the hotel. Tonight, if all went well, he was going to borrow that card. With luck and timing, she'd never know it was missing.

He just had to keep his wits about him, and not get carried away.

HE CAME OUT OF the bedroom with damp hair, and an open shirt.

The urge to run was so strong, Mercy actually got to her feet. She felt foolish for being there, unequipped to handle the situation, and yet, she would not let herself back away.

This was fear. Not because she thought Will would do anything to hurt her, but because she'd been running for so long it was terrifying to stop. If nothing else, she was going to do this just to prove she could. Because if Janice Foster and Piper Devon thought she was worth fighting for, could she believe any less?

"I'm worth this," she whispered.

"Pardon me? I didn't hear you." Will came closer, flicking an errant strand of hair off his forehead.

"Nothing. Just it's such a beautiful suite."

"It is." He stopped when he was across the coffee table. "I'm going to fix myself a scotch on the rocks. What can I get you?"

"I don't really drink much. And when I do, it's girly drinks. Usually with umbrellas."

He smiled, making her swallow hard.

"Let's see what they have in this exceptionally well-stocked bar."

She took a deep breath, then joined him at the far corner of the room, which was dedicated to eating and drinking. There was every kind of liquor she could imagine lined up on glass shelves with mirrors behind them. Gorgeous bottles that were pieces of art. Then there were snacks. Not just fruit, which was represented in abundance, but candy, crackers, popcorn for the nearby microwave, pretzels, cans of smoked oysters and so much more it made her dizzy, and he hadn't even opened the fridge.

"Ah," Will said. "Here it is." He pulled up a blender from just underneath the long bar. "I can't promise they have tiny umbrellas, but I could whip you up something girly. How about a piña colada? Or a strawberry daiquiri?"

"Sure. That would be great."

He grinned before he opened the fridge. Inside there were mixes, including the fruity drinks he'd mentioned and some chocolate ones, too. "Any preference?"

"Piña colada, I think."

"Good choice." He pulled out the mixer, got the rum from the bar, then some ice cubes, and put them all in the blender. To no one's surprise, there was a real pineapple in the fruit basket, which he cut like a pro.

Five minutes hadn't gone by and the blender was whirring away. He poured himself his scotch, but didn't taste it.

Buster had found the noise upsetting, however, so Mercy scooped him up. She distracted him with one of the treats in her pocket, and that, plus a tummy rub, kept him happy.

Finally, the drink was made and poured, a nice slice of pineapple was added, a straw dipped in. He took Buster, put him on the floor, then handed her the drink.

He lifted his scotch. "To surprises."

She tapped his small glass. "May they all be happy." Her first sip was wonderful. So wonderful, she took another, and a third.

"Good?"

"Yummy."

"Good. Now. Have you had dinner?"

"I ate something earlier, but go ahead and eat. I don't mind."

"No. I'm fine. Why don't we take our drinks to the living room. We'll talk about Buster, and how I'm going to make him the best dog in Wichita."

Mercy hadn't exactly forgotten the reason she'd ostensibly come to see Will, she was just sorry he hadn't. The drink, even those few sips, had given her strength. And God, he was so good-looking it was not fair. On her best day she wasn't close to being that gorgeous.

Will stepped around the bar and put his arm over her shoulder. "What's that frown about? I can get you something else—"

"No, no. I'm fine. I was just… Nothing."

"Okay. Come. Sit."

She walked more quickly to the couch.

Will cleared his throat then waited for her to take a seat on the couch. When she was settled, he looked back at Buster by the window. "Buster, come."

Mercy realized her mistake instantly. She blushed, of course, but as for running and hiding? Screw it. She just took another drink of pineapple-coconut goodness.

Buster obeyed, just as she had, but he wasn't as good at sitting. It took Will several tries and several treats for Buster to do as he was asked.

She just sat back and watched, enjoying the interplay. For the first time maybe ever, she was more interested in the man than the dog. Every move he made was smooth. He never raised his voice and even his praise was spot on. He kept walking across the large living room, calling Buster, asking him to sit. She could have watched him forever, but as the lights of the city became the dazzling backdrop, Will gave Buster a last treat, then came to the couch. "May I?"

Mercy nodded. Her heart was at it again, beating fast and hard. His hair had dried, but that stubborn lock was still dipping over his forehead. Before she could even think twice, she pushed his hair back.

His slow smile made all sorts of things happen inside her. Long dormant, her body came alive with a want that was warm and exciting.

He moved closer to her, and she could smell his clean skin, feel his warm breath on her face. Her eyes fluttered shut seconds before his lips touched hers.

She'd kissed him before, but not like this. Not with

anticipation coursing through her. Again, he moved slowly, gently, letting her get used to the idea. She was the one who parted her lips, asking him for more. He obliged quickly, easing his tongue between her lips, brushing her teeth. The moment her tongue touched his, it was as if a switch had been flicked. The gentleness of a second ago was gone. His hand went to her neck to hold her steady as he thrust, his mouth now hungry and demanding. Mercy gave as good as she got, adjusting her body on the couch until they were perfectly aligned.

The rest of the world disappeared until they were the only two, until he took over all her senses. Emboldened and eager, she touched his back, the side of his chest, letting her hands roam where they would.

He returned the favor, slipping his hand underneath her Hush jacket, pulling her white blouse out of her pants so he could brush his fingers over her bare flesh.

For a long time, they explored each other, and it was the stuff of her dreams. She loved kissing, although before now it had been mostly in her imagination. The others, and there hadn't been many, had been awkward, relentless. This was like the kisses in the movies, and she could almost hear the music swelling in accompaniment.

His hand cupped her breast and instead of stiffening up, instead of wanting to run, she leaned into him, wanting more. He flicked his thumb over her nipple, and it was electric even with her bra in the way.

Will pulled back. "I want to take you to the bedroom," he whispered.

She nodded.

"Sure, now? If it's too much—"

She pulled his hand out from under her blouse and stood. "Please," she said.

He didn't ask again. Instead, he took her hand and led her to the bedroom door, past the bundle of Buster, who was sound asleep on the carpet.

The huge bed looked to Mercy like an island of comfort, of promise. Will tossed off the decorative pillows and pulled down the comforter to reveal soft, pale sheets. She shivered in anticipation, but her stupid shyness made her blush at the thought of undressing.

Will turned off the bedroom lights, leaving the lights from the bathroom on so they could still see, just not glaringly. It helped. He slipped off his shoes and came to her, pulling her into his arms.

Mercy thought he was going to kiss her, but he just looked into her eyes. "You okay?"

"Nervous."

"Is that all?"

"No. Excited, too. I haven't done this in a while."

"I want to make you happy."

She met his gaze squarely, already feeling better. "I believe you."

He kissed her gently on the lips. "I would never do anything to hurt you."

"I believe that, too."

"I want you to remember this night as something sweet. Something great."

"We're off to a good start. Just… I don't know a lot of fancy moves."

He chuckled. "I'm not looking for fancy. I want to be close. To help you feel good. And safe."

She sighed. "That sounds perfect."

He slipped her jacket off, letting it fall to the floor. "I already think you're beautiful. Seeing you naked is a bonus."

"I wouldn't get too excited."

"Too late."

She let him unbutton her blouse, which he did amazingly gracefully, more so than she would have. She figured he'd go for her bra next, but he didn't. He undid her pants instead, but that was more awkward from his position, so she took over. Her shoes came off next, but she stopped at bra and panties.

He stepped back. Keeping his gaze locked on hers, he stripped. He didn't stop, though, and a moment later he was naked before her.

She'd been right about his body. He was stunning. All lean muscle and sinew, not quite as ripped as a movie star, but not far off. She couldn't help looking at all of him. He'd told the truth about his excitement. His cock was already hard. It was thrilling and naughty to see him so erect. He was beautiful there, too. Just right. Every inch of him.

Feeling brave, she reached behind her back and unsnapped her bra, letting it fall with the rest of her clothes. Her nipples were achingly hard. He didn't seem to mind that she wasn't very big. At least she wasn't drooping. No, from the look of things, he liked what he saw.

Her panties were next, and that took all her courage. Surprisingly, once she was completely naked, she relaxed. It was as if she'd passed some kind of test. Her reward was a look of hunger on Will's face that made her shiver.

"Why don't you get into that warm bed. I'll be right there."

It took her a second to move, but the sheets were an incredible treat. Silkier than she ever could have imagined.

She'd never understood why some sheets were hundreds of dollars. Now she did. It was amazing.

Will didn't come to the bed, however. He went to the big armoire, the one she knew was filled with all kinds of toys and treats.

She held her breath, hoping he wasn't going for something kinky, something she wouldn't know how to use, but no. He picked up a basket filled with condoms.

She relaxed and took the moment to look at his rear. She hummed in appreciation. Whatever Will did to keep in shape sure worked. There wasn't a thing wrong. Not one thing. Well, maybe that he was going to leave soon. Okay, she wasn't even going to entertain that thought, not for a second. This wasn't about forever. It was about tonight. This one night. No way she was going to get all sentimental about this.

She was going to have sex. With a gorgeous, nice man. This was what it was, and she was determined to make the most of it.

He turned. She threw back the covers. It was going to be fantastic.

9

WILL GAVE HIMSELF a moment to drink Mercy in. She truly was beautiful. Her long blond hair was finally out of her ponytail and it looked like spun silk on the pillow. As for her body—her legs were long and toned, her tummy flat. God, just looking at her hard little nipples made him hungry.

His gaze moved down to her trimmed little pussy. He liked that she wasn't shaved down there. It would have seemed fake, and there was nothing about Mercy that was anything but genuine.

For a man who'd been trained to read people, to hone in on any sign of a lie, Mercy was a vacation. She was simply who she was. Blushes and all.

Enough. He had to touch her. To taste her.

He climbed into the bed, glad she'd pushed the covers down. He wanted nothing to get in the way of his visual feast. His hand went to her stomach. He laid it flat, his palm just above her belly button, making her muscles tense. He waited as patiently as he could until they relaxed again. Only then did he lean over her, take her mouth, let himself feel the incredible smoothness of her skin.

Nothing was softer than women, and they didn't even know the power of that softness. To touch a woman's inner thigh was to find paradise. And it was nothing compared to the deep inside. When his cock slid home, when it was surrounded by that warm, wet perfect place, the world disappeared and he barely noticed. He wasn't the type to pray, but that made him give thanks to the genius who created women.

For now, though, he was letting his hands get all the glory.

As he deepened his kiss, he moved up until he cupped her small breast. It fit perfectly, her nipple a hard contrast, a sharp reminder of just how ready she was.

She moaned, which made him harder still. "Do you like that, Mercy?" he asked as he flattened his hand to rub his palm across her nipple. "Are you sensitive there?"

She moaned a yes that went straight to his cock.

"Tell me everything you like, everything you've ever desired. I want—"

"You," she said. "Just this. Just you."

He smiled and tweaked her other nipple. "Just me? Surely you deserve more than that."

She pulled her head back so she could look at him. "I feel like I've won a prize."

Her simple words made him stop his teasing. "What? No. Trust me, Mercy. I'm no prize. I've got problems, a lot of them. What you see here is the best part. The cream that rises. Be glad that you can't see below. It's not pretty."

"You're kidding, right?"

He shook his head, really wanting her to get this. Not that he wanted her to think too much about it, because that would spoil the fun, but she should know that she wouldn't miss a thing when he was gone.

Him, on the other hand? He was the one who was going to be sorry. He'd think about her on those empty nights, when the business was nothing but trouble, when his family… God, his family. They were the definition of trouble. Trouble he'd never handled well.

"There are a few things I do well," he said. "I'm good at my career. I know how to invest, and I know how to read people. And I know how to please you. Let me."

She smiled as she brushed her hand down his side as far as she could reach. Her grin turned wicked as she let that hand fall to his aching erection.

He hissed with her touch, and hoped like hell she wasn't going to play there long, because damn, he wanted this to last.

"Someone told me once, when a man said he was trouble, believe him."

"Wise words."

"I don't know. You seem pretty terrific from here."

"For tonight, let's go with that, huh? Let's just start at terrific and shoot for the moon." He kissed her, hard, then slithered down the bed, licking and nipping as he traveled down her body.

He parted her legs and got himself in position. Already, her scent was making him crazy. He ran his hands over her thighs until his thumbs brushed her lower lips. He opened her like a gift, all pink and moist and eager.

He leaned forward, making himself comfortable as he gave her a preview of what was to come. One long, flat-tongue lick that ended at her clit. She tasted like life. Salty, feral. Like a woman is supposed to taste.

He licked her again, and this time she wiggled

beneath him. One hand went to the top of his head where she tugged a little too hard, but that was okay. He was willing to lose some hair for the cause.

"Ohhh," she said, in a long, sweet sigh that got him busy. He closed his eyes, concentrating everything on his technique. He was good at it because he liked it. It was clear from the way she moved, the way she moaned, that Mercy liked it, too.

Weren't they a pair. Both of them so busy with their work they didn't take a moment to come up for air. Well, this should blow the cobwebs out of both their lives.

He pointed his tongue and circled her clit, moving faster and faster, riding her like a drugstore pony. He knew what she was after…but he wasn't going to give it to her, not yet.

He put his left hand on the side of her ass, and oh, yeah, she was close to liftoff by the way she trembled. He thought of taking a break, drawing it out, but this was Mercy, and he only wanted to tease a little bit.

In fact, it was time. With a deep breath, he made his tongue circles smaller and smaller until he was right there. The magic spot.

He should have put his condom on before he'd come down on her. It was especially sweet if he could be inside her as her orgasm was still making her constrict.

Ah, well. They had the night in front of them. If he didn't blow just from hearing her gasp, there was a good chance he'd feel everything he wanted to.

Her voice went up. And up. Good thing this was a fine hotel with thick walls, because shy little Mercy had a pair of lungs on her.

He smiled, but he didn't stop. He wasn't circling anymore. Just moving the point of his tongue as fast as he could. Yeah, his jaw ached, but that was fine by him. Besides, she was close. So damn—

"Oh, shit!" she cried, lurching out of his grasp. "Oh, my God."

He sat back on his haunches, not wanting to leave her, although he could see she didn't miss him. Not at the moment. She'd curled her legs up to her belly and her head was rolling from side to side on the pillow.

He could have taken care of himself no problem, just from watching her. But he let himself ache. He couldn't take his eyes off her blush. For once, it wasn't because she was embarrassed. That had to count for something.

MERCY KEPT GULPING air as she rode out the storm. An incredibly wonderful storm. She'd never come like that from any guy doing that to her. Honestly, she'd never particularly liked it before, and now she knew why. She'd been with bumbling idiots. Men who should have their dicks revoked.

"Oh, my God," she said, again, because she couldn't be bothered to find anything better. Why, why had it taken so long for her to discover this incredible feeling?

With a sudden burst of energy, she sat up, yanked Will by the shoulders and kissed him.

She tasted herself on his lips, which assured her once more that she was okay, but who cared? He needed praise. Applause.

He laughed while she was kissing him, and oddly she wasn't insulted. But she did pull back. "What?"

"Was it good for you?"

He was teasing her. She didn't mind. "So-so."

The look on his face!

A second later, he got it. That she could give tit for tat. "Oh, you are a devil."

"I didn't mean to hurt your feelings."

He tackled her, taking them both down. "Sweetie, I was there. I know what kind of time you had."

"So why did you ask?"

"I'm a guy."

"Oh, right."

He lifted up and put his head on his hand so he could look at her. "Remind me next time to give you something to hold on to. Something other than my hair, or what I have left of it."

She squeezed her eyes shut, remembering how she'd tortured him. "Sorry."

"Are you? Really?"

A quick peek made her waffle on her answer. Whatever he planned looked like it would be fun.

He sat up, grabbed her underneath her knees and lifted her legs in the air. "Are you?" he asked again.

"I'm not sure."

"Hmmm." He kept her legs up as he maneuvered around, then pushed them even higher on her chest. A second later, she felt a sharp slap on her butt, making her squeal. "Hey!"

His hand, the one that had just slapped her, was rubbing her now. The ache was turning into a surprisingly pleasant warmth. "Hey," she said, again, only this time, she wasn't complaining.

"I knew there was a wild woman in there," he

murmured. He put her legs down and came back up to join her. "You might fool all of them, Ms. Jones, but I see the animal in you. I see it when you don't think anyone's watching."

"Really? I don't think so."

He ran the back of his fingers down her cheek. "Oh, yeah. It's there. You've just been caged for a long, long time."

Unexpected tears came to her eyes and she quickly blinked them back. She wasn't even sure why his words affected her. They were in bed. That was another lesson she'd learned—men say all kinds of things without their pants on, and woman would be well advised to listen with half an ear.

He kissed her again, lightly at first, then deeper, with a clear message that the talking was over. His hand went to her breasts, teasing one nipple then the other. He stopped, but only to bring her hand to his cock. It wasn't quite as hard as it had been before, but Mercy knew how to take care of that.

She stroked the length of him, slowly, feeling him swell. His moan told her she was doing it right, but then she'd already known that.

Funny, with Will, she wanted to draw things out, not speed things up. Mostly before, her goal had been to finish. Not that she hadn't liked sex, but to be honest, she preferred taking care of herself, in her tiny little bed at home. All the men before Will had been eager to finish, too. Wham, bam, but rarely a thank you, ma'am.

This was a completely different experience. Maybe it was the fancy sheets, or that piña colada, but she didn't think so. Bottom line, she hadn't liked the men she'd slept with all that much. There were a lot of reasons she'd done what she'd done, but none of it had been close to this. She liked Will so much. Aside from the pretty, which was a nice bonus, but not the main point, he'd been kind. Attentive. Generous. And besides, the dogs liked him.

Just look at how Buster was already in love with Will. Thank goodness he lived near his nephew, so he could visit. Buster would miss him.

She would miss him.

"Mercy?"

She snapped back. "Sorry."

"You got kind of sad. Is something wrong?"

"No. Everything's fine. Everything's wonderful."

"Then you won't mind if I ask you to stop squeezing quite so enthusiastically?"

She opened her hand with a gasp. "Oh, God, did I hurt you? Are you all right?"

He laughed. "I'm fine. It wasn't that bad."

"I got to thinking—"

"You got distracted, and that's my fault. It won't happen again." To prove his point, he nudged her legs apart and then he touched her there, dipping two fingers inside her.

She inhaled sharply at the very pleasant intrusion. "That's so…"

"Is it now?" he whispered, his voice all sexy and low. "How about this?"

His fingers moved to her still sensitive clit. She winced, expecting pain, but he didn't hurt her at all. In fact, the gentle caress felt wonderful. Exciting. "Uh-huh," she said, as her eyes fluttered closed.

He surprised her with a kiss to her breast, and then his lips sucked in her nipple. She sighed and squirmed as he did things to her. Naughty things that felt just amazing.

By the time she remembered he deserved some amazing, too, he was hard as could be. Hard and hot, and if he didn't do something about it soon—

"Wait," he said, then he was gone.

She felt him turn over, heard him grab a condom and rip the package open. She kept her eyes closed, and since he was occupied, used her own fingers to continue where he'd left off.

"Oh, jeez," he said, although it was more of a moan than words. "That is just gorgeous."

She spread her legs a little bit more, knowing he was watching. Liking that he was watching.

"Have Mercy," he whispered.

She laughed, but she didn't stop. In fact, she moved her fingers more quickly, just like she did when she was alone. This was the most private thing, the one thing she'd never dreamed she'd reveal, and here she was, ready to come because Will was there, Will thought she was sexy. Because of Will.

She bucked as the first spasm hit, and before she could exhale, he'd snatched her hand away. He was between her legs in a heartbeat, holding her legs, spreading her wide. A second later, he was inside her, stealing her breath even as she cried out.

He went deep, filling her, pushing her, and it was unbelievable. She spasmed again, making him groan and thrust harder.

She grabbed for him, but couldn't reach, so she fisted the sheets instead. Every muscle in her body was tense and straining, wanting every bit of him. Needing him to swallow her completely.

He pulled out until he was barely there, then slammed back, pushing her whole body up the bed. Again, and she would have screamed if she could have found her voice.

Then, he slowed. He wound it down, making the anticipation as exquisite as the relief. He kept her on the edge, kept her guessing, and when she opened her eyes she met his burning gaze as he built up with speed and fierceness until she thought she would go mad.

Just as his rhythm became jerkier, less controlled, he put one of her feet down next to him, freeing his right hand. He found her clit once more, this time with his thumb, and he rubbed her as he thrust. The smooth moves were gone, but it didn't matter because he was getting her there. It wasn't difficult. She was so close that even with all that was going on she had to lift her hip as she held on so tightly she pulled the sheet halfway off the bed.

She came again, so hard she saw stars behind her eyelids. So hard her head banged against the headboard. He stopped then, not by choice, she thought, but because he came, too. His face scrunched up, his neck muscles strained, his whole body stiffened and with a growl that made her shiver, he kept on coming, pressing into her like a wild creature.

When it was over, when all that was left were trembling limbs and gasps for breath, he fell next to her. They were both sweating, their chests were heaving, and Mercy laughed right out loud. She had gone to the moon, the stars. Certainly she hadn't stayed on this old Earth.

She felt him laugh before she heard him. They did that for a long while, even though it made it harder to catch their breaths.

When she finally wound down, his head and hers shared a pillow. His body wrapped around hers, making her feel safe and happier than she could remember.

"You're amazing," he said.

"Me? I just went along for the ride."

"Oh, no." He rubbed her arm with a feather-light touch. "So responsive. So eager."

"So exhausted."

"Well, yeah. Hey, would you like something to drink? I'm parched."

"More than I can say."

He gave her a quick kiss on the temple, then he was up, surprising her with his energy. He wasn't gone long. First, to the bathroom, where she heard him use the sink, then over to the counter in the bath area, where he picked up two bottles of water.

He uncapped hers on the way back. By the time she'd hoisted herself into a sitting position, he was next to her, and they each polished off half their bottles. It tasted like heaven, and she gasped like a long-distance runner when she lowered the bottle.

"You can stay?" he asked.

"I want to. But I'd have to get up really, really early."

"That's okay."

"Wait. Buster."

"What about him?"

"You think he's slept all this time? Who knows what he's chewed on. Oh, man. I have to go—"

"You," he said. "Sit. Stay. I'll go get him."

"Be careful. He might have really made himself at home."

"Good point."

Naked, his hair a riot of disorder, he got out of bed once more. She watched his butt the whole way over to the door, and was sorry when he passed out of view.

This time, he was gone longer, and she imagined it wasn't quite the relaxing aftermath he'd been hoping for. When he came back, Buster was all wiggly in his arms, and when the dog saw her, she knew they weren't going to get to sleep anytime soon.

She should go. Take Buster to PetQuarters. She had a place to sleep there where she wouldn't have to disturb Will at the crack of dawn.

Man, she didn't want to, though. The thought of sleeping next to him was more enticing than any dessert. But she wouldn't complain. It was still her best night ever.

He'd promised her good memories, and he'd sure delivered. He'd also set the bar so damn high, she was probably going to curse the man long after he'd checked out. But she wouldn't think of that now. She'd just play with Buster for a while. Laugh with Will. Touch him just because she could.

Then she'd go back to her real life, although she doubted she'd ever be the same.

10

MERCY CHECKED the hallway before leaving Will's suite. It was late…well, early. Four-thirty on a morning that had looked beautiful from the fourteenth-floor windows. It would have been nice to sleep in. Share some coffee with Will. Shower together in that huge, unbelievable shower. But she wasn't going to focus on the regrets, right?

The only thing that troubled her was that she hadn't told him she was leaving. In fact, she'd waited for him to fall asleep. After watching him looking so serene and gorgeous, especially because Buster had curled up right by his head and the two of them were cuter than anything, she'd slipped on her clothes and picked up Buster, and he hadn't stirred.

He knew she couldn't stay. If someone caught her coming out of his room it would have meant big trouble, which would have blown her life up as effectively as a land mine. Gilly had assured her that she knew plenty of hotel employees who stayed over with guests, and Mercy supposed she'd chosen to believe her even though the risk was so high.

It had been worth it, though. She ached in places

she'd forgotten about, which should have been a problem but wasn't. The reminders were wonderful. The longer she could hold on to the night, the better.

Buster wiggled a bit on the elevator, but he was so sleepy he settled down right away. At the twentieth floor, she checked the hallway again, not really expecting to see anyone. Sure enough, it was empty, and she made her way to PetQuarters just fine.

The moment she walked in, it occurred to her she should have come up with some kind of story for Eddy and Andrew. They were used to her spending the night at work, but not sneaking in before dawn.

Oh, well. If they asked, she'd just tell them something had happened at her place and she had to get out. They'd buy it—they knew where she lived.

First, though, Buster needed to be put in his suite. As quietly as she could, she gave him a little kiss and put him on his bed. After tiptoeing out, she headed for the back room and a shower, stopping first at her locker to get some clean clothes.

Thankfully, both of the guys were sound asleep, which let her relax for the first time since she'd left Will's bed. As far as the rest of the world knew, nothing had happened. But she knew everything had changed. For the first time in her life she saw the possibility that she could find real happiness outside of work. Not with Will, of course. But with someone.

As the warm water of the very utilitarian shower washed away the evidence of her extraordinary night, she held tight to her newfound hope even as she fought the urge to pretend that Will wasn't going to leave her.

WILL WOKE TO SILENCE and an empty bed. It was just after seven, and even though he knew better, he hoped that Mercy was somewhere in the suite.

Still tired and a little achy, he looked on the floor. Only his clothes were there. Buster was gone, too. That damn little dog had made a mess on the beautiful tile floor in the living room, but Will still had a soft spot for the mutt. And an even softer one for Mercy.

What a night. She'd been…

He called room service and ordered breakfast, then climbed into a nice hot shower. As he washed, he replayed the whole thing, from start to finish, lingering over some of the highlights. No surprise, he had to take care of his hard-on. In fact, he couldn't imagine beating off to anything else, ever again.

But there was a downside to having such a great night.

It wouldn't be long until Drina made her move. Once that was taken care of, he'd be out of here. Back to his place, work, a life that had all of the trimmings but none of the meat.

He'd known for a long time that there was something missing. He'd even toyed with the idea of seriously searching for a partner. But when he got to the part where he'd have to talk about his background, his family, he slipped right back into his holding pattern.

Not that he thought no woman would ever accept him if she knew who he really was. Just not the right woman. He always thought of that old Groucho Marx bit—he wouldn't want to belong to any club that would have him for a member.

But maybe he'd been too narrow in his definition of the right woman. It wasn't easy to see a woman like

Mercy feeling comfortable at the opera or a political fund-raiser. A woman like Mercy would be great to come home to though. Maybe she'd even have a dog like Buster.

But the bald fact was he'd struggled his whole life to become the man he was. Respected, influential, wealthy. A man of standing in the community. He knew all too well how damaging the wrong spouse could be. It was enough that he had to hide his past. He didn't want to hide his future, too.

He got out of the shower and dressed. Room service arrived soon after, and he ate as he read the *Times,* despite the fact that his concentration was shit. By eight-thirty he'd checked his e-mail and called the office. The Parker installation had gone to hell and he'd yelled at Anita, which she hadn't deserved. He hung up angry and unsettled.

He needed to get to the bottom of the whole Drina disaster. Goddamn her. He should just leave. Wash his hands of the whole business and be done with it. It wasn't worth all this nonsense.

He put on his jacket then took the master key card he'd borrowed from Mercy. If he left, he wouldn't need to get it copied. It wasn't an easy process, and there was only one guy he knew who could do it. The copy would cost Will a small fortune, and for what? He should just go up to PetQuarters and slip this back into Mercy's jacket.

He stuffed the card in his pocket and cursed as if he were back on the street. Then he went off to get the damn card duplicated.

"YOU SPENT THE NIGHT with him."

Mercy spun around to glare at Gilly, already feeling

her face burning. "Shut up," she said, hissing at her used-to-be friend.

"No one's here," Gilly said, grinning. "Come on. You have to tell me every single detail."

"I do not."

Gilly took Mercy by the arm and dragged her all the way across the main floor to Mercy's office, where Gilly slammed the door, pushed Mercy into her chair and folded her arms. "Spill. You owe me."

"Gilly, don't be ridiculous. I have no idea what you're talking about."

"Liar!" Gilly dropped her arms and pouted so extravagantly it almost made Mercy laugh. "Sweetie, come on. Tell me you aren't glowing. Glowing! And look at your chin. If that isn't stubble burn than I'm not the woman I think I am, and we both know that's not true."

Mercy's hand went to her chin. She hadn't even noticed anything different about her face, but then she'd barely looked in the mirror as she was getting ready for the workday. It did feel a little sensitive, but that was beside the point. Talking about her private life had always been difficult for her. Gilly was usually the exception, but last night had been so special... It was as if talking about it would make it seem ordinary.

"Seriously, Merc. What's going on? Did he hurt you?"

"No. No, he was fine. Great. He was nice and it was just a really nice time. Well, maybe better than nice. You know. Nice."

Gilly leaned back and lowered her eyebrows. "Are you kidding me? Tell me you are, because honey, this was just supposed to be a one-night wonder. He's leaving. He's going back to Ohio or wherever. You were not supposed to fall for the guy."

Mercy stood up, ready to clock Gilly where it hurt most. "Would you stop? Nobody's fallen for anybody. Jeez."

Gilly sighed and rested her butt on the desk. "Oh, man. Now I feel totally guilty. If I'd known you were going to get all caught up in this I never would have encouraged you."

"Stop it. I'm telling you I'm not in love with him."

"If you aren't, you're one conversation away. I can see it in you, kiddo. You might be able to hide from most everyone up here, but I can tell last night was not just a good lay. It was a good lay, though, right?"

Mercy blushed. "I can't talk to you about this."

"Which just proves my point. Okay. We don't have to talk about it, not if you don't want to, but you'd better be damn careful. All it was supposed to be was sex. Nothing more. Getting your rocks off, then saying adios. If there's anything else going on, which we both know there is, then you'd better take a giant step back. Because no matter what, he's out of here. Gone. History. And you have to stay. With everything you have going on in your life, you do not need to add a broken heart. I'm just sayin'."

"Thanks for the advice. I'll keep it in mind." Mercy went to the door and didn't look back as she headed straight to the front desk. She needed to catch up on some paperwork, which was a good thing. It would keep her nice and busy. And keep her from thinking about what Gilly had said.

For God's sake, she wasn't in love. Not even almost in love. A few harmless fantasies didn't mean a thing.

She'd wanted to build a memory, and that's what she'd done. Nothing more.

The tightness in her stomach was nothing. Lack of sleep, that's all. Same for the lump in her throat.

She was not in love with Will Desmond.

WILL GOT A PERFECT table at Amuse Bouche. A combination of a reservation made by the concierge and a fifty slipped into the eager hand of the restaurant host had him in a nice dark corner, one with an excellent view of the rest of the patrons.

He wished Mercy was with him. He'd left several messages until he'd finally given up. She'd probably gone home early to catch up on her sleep. Still, it would have been nice.

He'd ordered the roasted capon with the 2002 Olivier Leflaive Meursault, then sat back as he scoped out the place. There were too many screens behind which diners might hide, but Drina preferred an audience, so he didn't worry overmuch. If she did come in, she'd find a center table and she wouldn't look back here.

He could see a couple of movie stars, young ones he recognized vaguely but couldn't put a name to, and there were a great many good-looking couples, all of them seeming pleased to be there. No, one couple was clearly in the midst of an argument, fairly exploding with bitter silence. But on the whole, these were eager participants in a show that was better from the inside. See and be seen.

He was surprised he'd waited so long to come to this restaurant. It was just the kind of place he normally frequented. It paid to be in the thick of things, especially at a hotel. One of the first things he'd done after he'd checked in was to find out who supplied the equipment for Hush's gym. They bought a good line, but he could do better. He planned on designing a pitch when he went back to work. Something Piper Devon couldn't pass up.

He didn't want to think about work. Or Drina, for that matter. Will had wasted the whole damn day on the key card. Something he still felt guilty about. He needed to get the original back to Mercy before she discovered it was missing. If she hadn't already.

Damn Drina. She caused him more problems than his business ever could.

He rubbed the back of his neck, trying to get the kinks out. He needed to do some catching up on his own sleep. Last night had wrung him out, albeit in a good way. But he wasn't seventeen anymore.

"Mr. Desmond?"

He looked up, startled at his waiter's appearance right next to his table. Instead of his wine, he had a drink—whiskey it looked like—on his tray. Will opened his mouth to tell him he'd made a mistake, when the waiter put the drink down.

"Compliments of your grandmother," he said.

Will looked past the waiter into the center of the dining room. Shit. There she was. He should have known she'd want to be backlit. Will shook his head as he studied her perfect silver hair, her arched brows, her infamous décolleté. She'd worn a dress he'd seen infrequently, emerald-green that went with her necklace, with her eyes. She laughed and the sound had lost none of its magic.

Her companion looked suitably dazzled. Will didn't recognize him. He clearly had money. No one got to his age and looked that good without careful tending and upkeep. The white hair had been neatly trimmed, his suit unquestionably not off the rack, and he looked at Drina as if he'd sign away his family yacht if she would just laugh again.

Will sighed, wondering who the man was. How Drina had pulled him into her web. But mostly, Will wondered just how bad it was going to get. If Drina had reinforcements, things could get tricky.

The waiter shuffled a bit. "She requests that after dinner…" He cleared his throat and looked in Drina's direction. "She asked me to say this precisely, sir. That after dinner, you and your interference go jump off the Brooklyn Bridge."

Will bit down on a curse. "She actually said a few more choice words, didn't she?"

"Yes, sir. And she also told me to charge you for her dinner."

"Did she order the Veuve Clicquot?"

"Yes, sir. The 1988."

"That's fine. Thank you."

The waiter bowed and headed back to the safety of the kitchen.

Will picked up the whiskey and held it up to his dear grandmother. She smiled and gave him the Princess-of-Airs nod. Then she went back to her beau and Will sipped his drink, which was at least twenty years old and would cost him an arm and a leg.

If she thought her little trick would send him scurrying… No, of course she didn't. Drina might be a pain in the ass, but when she set her mind to something, she was like a bulldog.

His grandmother was a product of her culture, which sounded great, comforting even, until one realized her culture was a mix of Romanian Gypsy folklore and superstition combined with a family tradition of con artistry that had begun in the 1920s, blossomed in the '40s and come truly into its own in the '60s and '70s.

His own parents, now deceased, had been consummate grifters. They, along with their cousins, uncles, aunts and relatives of dubious birth, had practiced their art with as much flair and dedication as the most renowned maestros. New York had been their playground, and marks from around the world had provided their bounty.

As Will sipped the excellent whiskey, he thought of the countless hotels throughout his childhood, the many pockets he'd picked, the hundreds of sad tales he'd spun to the hapless, who would never, even if he'd been caught, believe that a child could be so deceitful.

His real education hadn't been reading, writing and arithmetic. It had been the long con, the short con, the art of the pickpocket. He'd learned early and well how to case a place, how to pick a mark, how to use his innocence to reel in a soft-hearted soul.

It was a hell of a legacy. One that had ruined his siblings, sent his parents to prison and early deaths. It had chased him through school, and well into college. He'd done everything in his power to disassociate himself from his past. The only fly in the ointment was Drina. And a promise Will had made to his grandfather.

The waiter came back, this time with his wine, but Will changed his order. "Bring me another," he said, holding up his almost empty glass.

"Yes, sir."

That damn promise. Marius had been dying. In prison, where all the male members of Will's family seemed to end up. Marius had pleaded with him, made him swear on his mother's grave. Threatened to curse him if he didn't keep his word.

It had seemed relatively simple back then. Watch over Drina. Make sure she didn't get in trouble. And do whatever it took to keep her from ending up like Marius.

Had his grandfather realized that he'd cursed Will no matter what? That watching out for Drina had cost him time, money, energy and too many reminders of a bad past? The woman was never repentant. Just angry at him for spoiling her fun.

She was still proud of the old ways. She couldn't see that they'd hurt people, hurt their own. All she cared about these days was honoring Marius's memories. Why stealing a dog collar, diamonds or no, would be an honor to a dead man made no sense, and never would.

And still, Will couldn't walk away. He was tempted. Over and over again. But he would keep his word. He would keep Drina out of jail. This time.

Who was he kidding? He'd do it as long as it was necessary. He shouldn't have an ounce of loyalty left in his blood, but there it was. His family.

His whiskey arrived, and it occurred to him that

things could have been worse. Mercy could have been there to see it. She would have been all questions. It would have been awkward. He didn't speak about his family. Not now, not ever. Not even to Mercy, who had her own miserable past.

For a moment, he wondered what would happen if— No. Not even her.

11

IT WAS ALMOST FIVE, and Mercy touched the cell phone in her pocket for maybe the hundredth time. Will had left six messages since yesterday. It had been incredibly difficult to heed Gilly's advice and not return his calls. Not that ignoring him was the answer. He was going to show up to see Buster, if nothing else, so Mercy would have to face him. The trouble was, she ached to see him.

Since her conversation with Gilly, Mercy had done a lot of thinking. She really wasn't in love with Will. But she wanted to be. That's what worried her. She wanted to be in love so badly it brought tears to her eyes. It was monumentally foolish, but it was true.

No one like him had ever come into her life. Her past had been a pretty big nightmare, one that didn't lend itself to happy endings. She'd beaten the odds ten-thousand-fold just to be where she was. Finding a way to make her love for animals pay, and in such a place, was huge. She'd found her brass ring. The odds of finding another were astronomical.

And yet, after all the disappointments—all those foster families that promised a normal life, men who wanted nothing more than to use her body for their own amusement—there was still a spark of the dreamer inside of her. She hadn't known it was there, and it made her feel stupid and vulnerable. Of all people, she should know that love was a romantic notion mostly unconnected to the real world. How many people did she know that were really in love? The forever kind. That would be a big fat none. Well, no, that's not true. Her friend Mia Traverse, she'd fallen in love with the detective who'd worked on the murder that took place in the hotel, and they seemed happy. But that had only been going on a couple of months. Would they be together in five years? Ten?

Maybe that wasn't fair. When the whole idea of marriage got started, people didn't live very long. They'd be together ten, fifteen years if they were lucky. Now, people were living past eighty, ninety. Wasn't it completely unrealistic to think two people could be together for fifty years?

She sighed and got serious about brushing Zoe. She was a beautiful Australian shepherd mix who loved her bath day. She also played dead if you said "Bang!" and woke up at "Resurrect!" So hilarious.

See? This is where she belonged. Right here in PetQuarters where none of the dogs would break her heart. Sure they would leave, but there were so many that she was always busy and happy, and she did her best to make sure the animals were, too. It was a worthwhile life. She made a difference. She still donated her time to the animal shelter, so she gave back and helped get dogs adopted to loving families.

This was the kind of love she could believe in. Not that fairy tale stuff. Gilly was right. What she'd had with Will was a fabulous night, but that's all. One night.

He'd delivered exactly as promised, and she needed to let it go at that.

"He's leaving soon," she whispered to Zoe. "His life is far away from here. I'll never see him again. It's what it was, right, girl?"

Zoe panted her agreement, and Mercy kept on brushing. But she still wanted to call him back. To stretch that one-night stand to two. To as many as she could as long as he was here.

The only problem with that was the ending. *He goes back to his life, she cries herself to sleep every night.* Not a pretty picture.

"You're here."

She spun around at the sound of Will's voice. He stood at the door of the grooming salon, gazing at her with troubled confusion. Simply looking at him made her tremble. His dark hair, those shoulders. She could look at him forever.

"I thought you might be sick."

She shook her head. "I'm sorry. I should have called you."

He walked toward her, the hurt quite clear on his handsome face. "Don't worry, I'm not here to bother you. I just came to see Buster, and find out if you were okay."

"You're not bothering me. I was rude and horrible not to call you."

"Don't worry about it. For what it's worth, I had a wonderful time last night. I'll never forget it. But I have no expectations. You didn't do anything wrong."

That made her feel even worse. "I had a wonderful time, too."

He smiled a little. "Did you?"

She closed her eyes, not willing to hurt him anymore, just because she was being an idiot. "It was unbelievable." When she looked at him again, she didn't blink or try to hide. She needed for him to know she was telling the truth. "I've never experienced anything like that before. Thank you. I won't forget it, either. Not ever."

"I'm glad," he said. "I think. I certainly didn't want to make you uncomfortable."

Chrissy walked in, accompanied by Daisy, a terrific little border collie mix. "Hi, Mr. Desmond," she said before turning to Mercy. "There's someone up front for you, Mercy."

"Okay. Can you finish Zoe or should I call Eddy?"

"I can do it. No problem."

Mercy put down the comb, not sure if she was pleased at the interruption or not. She needed to talk to Will. It wasn't fair to do otherwise. Now she realized she should have done it over the phone. The nearness of him made everything worse. Wanting him was a physical ache.

When she reached him she simply couldn't resist touching him. Just his arm, but it was enough to make it hard to breathe. "Can you wait?"

"I'll go see Buster."

She nodded and let him go.

The walk to the front desk was difficult. She wanted to turn, to look at him, but she kept her eyes forward. How could she be so caught up by this lust? It was lust, after all. Nothing more glamorous. Lust plus unrealistic fantasies that made it feel like something more.

Pumpkin's mother stood by the dog sweaters. She hadn't been to see Pumpkin for two days, which made

Mercy angry. Little Pumpkin could be a wonderful pet, if someone took the time to care for her properly. What would happen when Mrs. Dalakis went home? Would Pumpkin stand any chance for a happy life?

"Ah, you're here. I wanted to see Pumpkin, and ask you some questions."

"Of course, Mrs. Dalakis. I know she's missed you."

"I doubt that. I'm not proud of it, but there it is. That's what I wanted to talk to you about."

"Why don't you come back with me? We can talk in her suite."

Mrs. Dalakis nodded. She was once again dressed to the nines. Her hair was neat and elegant, her outfit— pale green silk pants, a green and white blouse, with a green duster—looked as if it had come from a designer's showroom. The woman had so very much. Was Pumpkin just an accessory, like poor Lulu?

She let the woman in and held the door for her. Mrs. Dalakis stopped for a moment at the door as if she'd forgotten something, then walked with Mercy to the pet suites.

Pumpkin went understandably nuts when she saw her mom, which made the woman's steps slow.

Mercy kept her face blank. It wasn't good for business to show her disdain for those who didn't treat their pets well. As far as she was concerned, it was a sacred duty. She had no patience for those who shrugged it aside.

They passed by Buster's suite, and of course Mercy looked. Will had Buster on his lap, belly up for a nice rub. Will, however, wasn't looking at Buster or her, but at Mrs. Dalakis. It was difficult to read him. He seemed, what—angry? Surprised? Because Mercy was paying attention to a guest? That didn't make much sense.

She opened Pumpkin's door and ushered the woman inside. Instead of going to her dog, Mrs. Dalakis stood in the corner, staring at her as if she'd never seen the dog before.

"Is something wrong?" Mercy asked, as she picked up the Chihuahua. Pumpkin continued to bark at her owner, but she stopped shaking once Mercy had her close against her chest.

"I fear I've made a mistake. I thought having a dog would be a comfort to me, after losing my husband. The truth is, I'm not suited to the task. I've never had a dog, a pet of any kind, really, and I had convinced myself that it wouldn't matter. Unfortunately for Pumpkin, it does. I wanted to talk to you about finding her a home where she could get the attention and care she needs."

Mercy exhaled a pent-up breath, and coincidentally, Pumpkin stopped barking. It was what she'd hoped. "I'll certainly see what I can do. I don't know anyone offhand, but I'm sure we can work something out."

"I won't be staying at the hotel much longer. A few days, perhaps. I know I have no business asking, but could you please wait until I've gone to show Pumpkin off? I'll be happy to take care of any expenses necessary to keep her here until you find her a home."

"Sure. We can do that."

The woman hesitated. "Is there any chance you can take her? She certainly likes you."

"I can't have a pet where I live."

"Well, that's a waste, isn't it?"

Mercy smiled, liking the woman so much better for having copped to her mistake. "It is." She gave Pumpkin a nice scratch under the chin. "I'll make sure she finds a wonderful home. Thank you."

"I'll leave her in your hands, then." Mrs. Dalakis opened the suite door, but stopped after two steps. "It occurs to me that I might actually know someone. Are you going to be here this evening?"

"I get off work in an hour."

"Someone will be here, though?"

"Yes. Dylan and Grace will be here all night."

"Thank you, Ms. Jones. You've been a big help."

"I'll see you out."

"No need. I know my way."

Mercy took her at her word and sat down with Pumpkin on the bed. "You hear that, sweetie? We're going to find you the best parents ever. Someone who wants you so, so much."

Pumpkin wiggled and gave her a little squeal, as if she understood. Maybe she just felt relief at not having to be with Mrs. Dalakis. Dogs were pretty smart about things like that.

She gave Pumpkin a treat, then took her out to the small-dog pen. She looked in Buster's suite, but Will wasn't there. In fact, Buster wasn't, either. He was already in the pen.

Mercy left Pumpkin to play with the others and went to her office, but Will wasn't there, either. He wasn't anywhere in the facility.

Was it payback for not picking up his calls?

At the thought, her cell rang. It was Will.

"Hey, I'm sorry I had to leave. I forgot I had to take

care of some business, but it won't take long. Will you be there in half an hour?"

"Yeah. Is everything all right?"

"Fine. Just a time-sensitive e-mail. I'll come back down soon, I promise."

"Good. We need to talk."

He sighed. "I guess we do."

Mercy hung up, already anxious for his return. At least this gave her a little while to figure out what she was going to say.

"DRINA, STOP."

"This is none of your business."

Will caught the door just before it slammed in his face. He'd followed Drina to her room, and the call to Mercy had cost him, but now he was here, and she was going to listen to him. He stepped inside and closed the door behind him. "I can't let you do this."

"You can't let me do what? Have a vacation? I'm entitled."

"You live forty minutes from here. If you wanted a vacation it wouldn't be to Manhattan."

"I can go where I want. You have no say."

"Drina, I know you're planning to steal that dog collar. I wouldn't give a damn, except I have no desire to visit yet another relative in prison."

"I'm still your grandmother. Show some respect."

"I want to, but how can I when you insist on pulling another heist. It's enough, *bunica*. It's not worth it."

Drina went to her desk and sat with her back straight, her head high. "It's worth everything."

"Why? Explain it to me, would you? Because I can't

see it. You don't need the money. Marius left you plenty, and if you need more I'll make sure you get it. So why? What's so important about this damn dog collar?"

"I'm not going to explain myself to you. You have no regard for me, for my life. You follow me like a cop. How long have you been here? You're so ashamed you couldn't have come to me? Why don't you just leave me be? If I make a mistake, I make a mistake. No need to dirty your hands."

"I can't leave you be."

"Why not? It would be a mercy to both of us."

"Because I promised. I swore to Marius that I would keep you safe."

She deflated then. As if all the air had left her body. Suddenly, she looked old. Unmasked. Defeated. "Marius would want me to do this."

"What, Drina? Do what? Steal from some idiotic people who don't have better things to do with their money? What possible reason could Marius have for wanting you to do that?"

She turned her face. "Please get out, William. I want to rest."

"Drina—"

"Go. Don't make me ask again."

He stared at her, surprised at his own emotions. For all of it, he still loved the old woman. She didn't make it easy, but he did. "I'm going to keep my promise."

"You'll do whatever you please, just as you always have."

He went to the door, unsatisfied and uncomfortable. But Drina was Drina. He wasn't going to change her. All he could do was try to mitigate the damage.

MERCY WAS OFF the clock, changed and waiting for Will. Instead of excited anticipation, all she felt was dread. She'd gone over and over what she could say to him, but nothing sounded right. She couldn't tell him the truth. Not that he wouldn't believe her, or that he'd make fun of her, but saying out loud what she could barely stand to think was too much.

She needed to distance herself. Let him know that it had been swell, but now it was over. Thanks so much for everything. The dinner. The talking. Showing her the difference between having sex and making love.

The elevator's ding brought her attention to the door, so when it eased open her problem was directly in front of her. Her body reacted without her consent. Flutters, quick breathing, the need to touch her hair as she blushed.

"Hey," he said.

"Hey." Her voice broke on the single syllable,

He held the elevator open with his arm. "Let's go."

She hesitated, and he saw it.

"Dinner," he said. "Only dinner. We'll have that talk."

She stepped in next to him, wishing the elevator was much, much larger.

He didn't say anything on the way down to the lobby, or try to touch her. Which was very nice and polite, but it was so hard.

She'd made love to this man. She'd been more intimate with him than anyone in her life. He'd been so sweet, so gentle. And God, how he'd made her come.

Of course she was falling in love with him. Who wouldn't? It astonished her that he wasn't married already. Maybe he was, who knew? Maybe he was married with five kids and she was his vacation fling.

No, she'd been exactly right. It was lust. Wishful thinking. What more could it be when she knew nothing about him? He'd given her the facade, and she'd filled in the rest. It wasn't his fault, but hers.

"I'll get a cab," he said. "One minute."

Will went to the doorman and gave him a tip. A moment later, they were on their way to the Village.

He sat pretty close to her, but again, he didn't try to touch her. What he did was bad enough. He looked at her as if she mattered. As if she had the power to hurt him, which seemed impossible. Not this man. He had everything going for him. She had...

He touched her hand. "Please, don't be sad. Whatever it is, it's okay. If I did something wrong, I'm sorry. I only wanted to make you happy."

Tears sprang to her eyes and she turned away from him, not willing to let him see. He was being too nice. She'd had a lifetime of dealing with mean, with ugly, and she knew how to handle that.

Nice threw her. Goddamn it, nice made her cry. Nice made her want what she could never have.

12

THE RESTAURANT was casual and good, but more importantly, it was quiet and there were booths where he and Mercy could talk without being overheard. No line, luckily, and no fuss as they were led to a table in the back.

He waited as patiently as he could for her to choose her dinner and drink, but when ordering was out of the way, his patience had all but run out.

"I'm really sorry I didn't call you back," Mercy said, her gaze on her hand around her water glass. "You didn't deserve that."

"It's all right."

She glanced at him, then away. "No, it's not. You've been nothing but great, and I was being selfish."

"Listen, Mercy. I've had an incredible time with you, but I understand. I'm leaving. You're staying. I'm as surprised as you that we connected like this. I can't say I'm sorry, either. But if you feel you should keep your distance—"

"I don't." She took a breath, letting it out slowly. "That's only partially true. I do need to keep my distance. You're a guest. I could lose my job."

He almost believed her. The words she'd said were technically true, but that wasn't the reason she was putting on the brakes. At least not the whole reason. "That would be a crime. You're much too good at it to put your job at risk. Everyone would lose."

She cleared her throat, still examining those fascinating fingers. "Thank you."

"That's it then. It's the job thing."

For a long time, she said nothing. He didn't push her, even though he wanted to. The truth was, she was right. He had gotten what he needed from Mercy, and if he were any kind of a gentleman, he'd leave her the hell alone. Leave her with the idea that he was a nice guy, a traveler from Wichita with a nephew who wanted a dog.

Shit, all he'd wanted to do was stop a robbery. Prevent an old woman from going to jail. So he'd had to get creative, so what?

He wished he understood exactly what it was that had made her upset. Was he wrong about their night together? It had been fantastic for him, and he'd thought for her. But then, she'd left so soon. No note, just gone. "Mercy, if I did something to upset you—"

"You didn't. I swear, I don't regret what we did, it's just better if—"

The waiter came with their food. They'd both ordered pasta, a beer for him, a soda for her. Nothing spectacular, not close to the food from Amuse Bouche, but good. He wasn't hungry in the least.

When it was just the two of them again, he tried to catch her eye. Mercy wasn't ready. There was no use forcing things. Either she'd tell him or she wouldn't.

He wished he could be straight with her. Tell her about Drina, about his family, about the dog collar, all of it. But it was way past that now. Drina was about to make her move. He had a key that would get him in anywhere he needed to be and he'd returned the original with Mercy none the wiser. He had access to PetQuarters because no matter what, Mercy would never stop him from playing with Buster.

He was even familiar enough with the facility to get in after hours. It would be easy at this point to say he wanted to spend some of the night hours with his dog. No one would say boo, and he felt sure he could stop Drina before things got out of hand.

He had a feeling, however, that she wouldn't go after the collar inside PetQuarters. She'd be smarter to make the move when the dog was on a walk. A moment's distraction, perhaps claiming her purse had been stolen, and when the dust settled, she'd be the first one to point out the missing diamonds. Drina could pull that one off without breaking a sweat.

The news would get back to PetQuarters in a heartbeat, and he'd be there to hear it. That's when he'd swing into motion, returning the collar with some bullshit explanation. No one would care once the owners had their precious jewels back.

Mercy had taken a few bites, but then put down her fork. She looked up at him, and he could see the determination in her expression. So pretty. So sad. He wanted to kiss her. To hold her close and assure her that everything would be okay.

"I've asked Gilly to take over training Buster. You can ask her when would be a good time to meet up."

"Gilly, huh."

"She's good. Really good. Buster already loves her to pieces, so you won't have any problems."

"But it won't be you."

"I think that's for the best."

"I understand."

"You gave me a night I'll never forget. Something I'll always treasure. But it was meant to be a one-night thing. You're going back to Wichita. And I have so much work to do. We keep getting more city dogs, which is great, but it means spending more time walking and grooming, well, you know…"

Will ate some pasta as he listened to Mercy, knowing everything she'd said after "going back to Wichita" was filler. Words that were meant to distract. She'd said everything in that one sentence. He was going back to Wichita.

It was true, too. Not literally. He was actually going back to SoHo, but in essence, he was leaving Mercy's world. They'd spent a lot of time together in just a few days, pushing the intimacy scale all the way off the charts. It was a lot for him to handle, and he had a lot more life experience than Mercy.

It was clear to him now that she wasn't saying goodbye because she'd had a bad time, or because he'd done something wrong. She wanted out because it had been so very fine.

He'd give her one thing—she was smart. The wisest thing she could do was cut and run. It wouldn't do either of them any good to get more involved. Not when the outcome was predestined. The kind of chemistry they had was meant for those with a future.

"I need for this to work so I can move out of my place. It's so horrible. I just hate my roommates and hate that they don't pick up after themselves, and I can't live in any apartment that doesn't allow pets."

"I can see that," he said. "You deserve to have a nice place to live."

"It's New York. That doesn't come easily."

He nodded. "You spend a lot of nights at Hush."

"Whenever I can. But I'm always afraid the wrong person's going to find out."

"Who would that be?"

She shrugged. "Janice Foster. She's the general manager. She's nice and all, but I don't think she'd want me spending so much time there."

"If you were my employee, I wouldn't mind. Someone responsible always watching the store? That's only a negative on your end."

"It's not though. I love it there."

"But it's not nearly enough. You deserve a full life, Mercy. Time to develop other interests. Time just to decompress and not think about work."

She shook her head. "It's the best thing I have."

He understood that. He'd buried himself in his work as well. Nothing was safer. There were definitive numbers in play. Profits and losses, units sold, orders taken. It was clean and it could all be spelled out in columns and pie charts. Nothing messy. Nothing illegal. No swindling, no cons. It was the exact opposite of his old life. He'd designed it that way. As far as the world knew, he'd never been a pickpocket. Never pulled a con and never made someone feel like a fool for having been scammed.

"This is good," Mercy said. "The food, I mean. It's a nice place."

"Yeah. Some friends recommended the place."

"You have a lot of friends in New York?"

"No," he said, the lie coming easily. He didn't even have to think about it. "Listen, Mercy. I get it," he said, changing the subject abruptly. "You need to put all your energy into PetQuarters. Me, I'm just a distraction, and you don't need that. I was selfish, taking up so much of your time."

"You weren't."

He smiled and leaned toward her. "Just know that you gave me a night I'll never forget. You're very special, Mercy. So amazing. I can still feel you on my fingertips. Still taste you."

Her blush appeared quickly and he thought of how that same flush spread when she came. He wondered if he'd ever see a woman blush without thinking of Mercy. That night was going to haunt him for a long time.

"Can I ask you something?"

"Anything," he said.

"Tell me the truth. Is it like that for you all the time? Don't worry, you won't hurt my feelings. I, just...I would like to know."

"God, no," he said. "God, no. I won't lie. There's not much about having sex that isn't pleasurable, but that night with you, that was off the charts."

She looked at him with a strong, steady gaze, trying to detect how truthful he was being. He wasn't worried because he wasn't lying. Not even a little bit. Missing Mercy was inevitable. He just hadn't wanted it to start so soon.

"Okay," she said, mostly to herself.

The waitress came by, but they both said no to dessert. It was time to go, but he didn't want to. Oddly, he'd miss the other parts of being with Mercy as much as the sex. Playing with Buster, watching her work her magic with the dogs. Just hanging out had been a nice change from his breakneck pace, and he knew very well that he wouldn't take the time to do it on his own.

Buster would go to a good family, someone from the office. Drina would go back to New Jersey and keep out of trouble, at least for a while. And he would do what he always did; only now, there would be this memory to haunt him.

He paid the bill and they went out to catch a cab back to Hush. He'd offered to see her home, but she'd declined. It was for the best. He hoped Drina would make her move soon, just so he didn't have to keep seeing Mercy. He preferred the quick-rip method, walking away without a look back.

The ride to the hotel was silent. But this time, he was a lot more aware of the woman sitting so close. He knew now how her shiny hair felt like silk, especially when it brushed his chest. Her scent was clean and fresh and her taste, well, that wasn't something any man could forget.

Shit, he had to stop thinking about it because he was getting hard. Not fatally, not yet, but if he didn't keep his mind off Mercy, he'd never be able to get out of the cab.

She kept darting glances his way. Her hands were in her lap. Her back was straight. But this time, when she looked, she blushed.

So he wasn't alone. It should have been funny, the two of them thinking about each other like that. But it wasn't amusing at all.

He wanted her so badly. He couldn't remember a time when he'd cared so much. She wasn't even his type, and yet she'd captivated him. The idea of making her come, of making her scream, swirled over and over in his head, becoming more and more urgent the closer they got to midtown.

Mercy sat up straighter, turning her body more toward the door.

He coughed, looked at the intersection, hoping they were almost there. He wondered if he should stop the cab and walk the rest of the way.

Images came to him of her breasts, the curve of her waist, the line of her neck. He could hear the way she gasped, the song of her orgasm.

The ride had to be over soon. It was taking too long, and he couldn't take it anymore.

She squirmed on the vinyl seat.

He averted his gaze.

Finally, they were coming up on the hotel. A few more minutes and he could go up to his room. Take a cold shower.

The cab turned a little too quickly. Mercy leaned a little too far. She touched his leg.

He looked at her hand, pale, perfect, expecting her to snatch it away. But the seconds ticked by. He looked up, right into her eyes.

He should have turned away. Made a joke. At the very least, he should have cleared his throat.

Instead, he pulled her into a kiss so desperate he thought the night would catch fire.

NO, NO, NO.

The word kept repeating in her head as her body rebelled, as she drowned in his arms, in his kiss.

It was crazy. She knew what would come of this.

Knew she would pay for this sin with pain and regret. It didn't matter. All her words were nothing, all the warning bells were silenced as they came together in the backseat of the cab.

His hands were on her back and she ached for them to be on her skin instead of her shirt. His tongue thrust into her mouth and it wasn't enough. She wanted more. She wanted to be naked and writhing as he filled her.

The sound of a stranger's "Hey" stopped her cold, and she jerked herself free, only then noticing the cab had stopped in front of the hotel.

"Come with me," Will whispered.

She couldn't look at him. If she did, she was done for. With all the strength she possessed, she threw open the door and forced herself out of the taxi. She ran inside the hotel, through the lobby, bumping into a guest without stopping to apologize. She made it to the elevator and counted the agonizing seconds as it took her to the twentieth floor.

She still didn't feel safe. The door to PetQuarters was locked, and it took precious time for her shaking fingers to get out her key card, to let herself in, to pass through the gate and into the back room. She didn't stop to speak to Grace or to look at the dogs as she sprinted to her office.

Once there, she closed the door, locked it and collapsed into her chair. Breathing hard, she told herself she'd done the right thing. That making love with Will would only hurt her worse. She'd been right. Mature. Sensible.

It didn't stop her body from aching, from needing his touch. All she felt was his absence. Where his hands weren't, where he should have been kissing her.

She wanted to scream from the unfairness of it all.

Why was it so hard? How could anything be as cruel? She was better off not knowing. Not feeling. It had been fine before she knew what she was missing. How empty her life was.

No one had told her it could be like that. No one should have.

HE SHOULD HAVE BEEN watching Drina. At the very least, the cold shower should have worked. But it hadn't, and he couldn't force himself to move.

She was gone. Whatever could have been with Mercy was over. It didn't help that he'd boxed himself in this corner. That his lies had made it impossible to pick up the phone, to call her, to beg her to reconsider.

She was right. She was much better off without him. He had no business involving her in his family trouble.

So he stared out the window, into the dark of the Manhattan night. Maybe if he drank enough, he'd get tired, fall asleep. He would face the truth tomorrow. But the liquor tasted like ash on his tongue.

He'd sleep on the couch tonight. He just couldn't face that empty bed.

DRINA HAD MADE IT inside PetQuarters without setting off any alarms. Even the dogs had ignored her as she had crept to the darkest corner to wait.

It wasn't too bad. There was a stool to sit on. Her equipment was in her lap. She was in shadows, keeping herself alert and calm with thoughts of Marius. She was used to spending long hours doing nothing. That had become so much of her life. Even with the television on, her home was just a place to sit. To wait. To remember.

She'd seen the concierge run through. Something bad had happened to her. Something to do with her heart. If Drina didn't know better, she'd swear it had something to do with William.

He had been such a good boy. The brightest light of all the grandchildren. He'd been an exceptionally skilled grifter, even as a child. No one doubted his innocence. He cried on command, and not crocodile tears, either. He could have done anything.

But he'd wanted nothing to do with the life. Once he got into his precious Harvard, paid for by the family that disgusted him, he'd turned his back on everything he'd known. The day he'd legally changed his name, Marius had wept.

It wasn't a typical life, but they weren't a typical family. Still, they had a code, an honor that outsiders could never comprehend.

Their lives all started to fall apart after William had gone to college. Her son had been tripped up by a sting operation. Her daughter-in-law had been swept up in the aftermath. It wasn't long until Joseph, William's brother, had fallen into drugs and death and his sister, Angela, had fallen into a cult.

Then the final nightmare. Her cousin, the bastard Cristescu, who had borrowed so much money from Marius, turned against them. He'd gone to the police. Tricked Marius. Sent him to die in prison.

The bastard Cristescu and his bitch of a wife created a new life for themselves, using Marius's money. It was all a fraud, a long con that was as deceitful and treacherous as anything Drina had ever seen.

It had taken her two years to untangle the web. To

discover all the partners, all the layers of lies. It had been what she'd lived for. To avenge her husband. To send Cristescu and his wife to prison. So they should know what Marius had lived through. So they should die in a cell. Like animals.

It was almost over. Soon she would have everything she needed. Then she would put things in motion, and in the end, she'd watch the police put them in handcuffs and she'd bake a cake.

The only one she was worried about was the concierge. She wasn't supposed to be there. But, Drina had faith. Tonight, all the stars were right, all the signals. So she would wait. Only, she didn't have to wait long.

The girl came out of the office and then back the way she'd come in. It was ten-thirty. Drina had no idea how long she would be there. She wasn't leaving until the job was done.

WILL WAS ON HIS THIRD whiskey, and he didn't feel a goddamned thing. He hadn't turned on a light. He didn't want to see. The couch was comfortable, but he wasn't tired. Thoughts of Mercy wouldn't leave him be.

He sighed as he watched a plane in the distance. Then he heard a knock.

His heart beat more quickly as he put down his drink. He tightened his robe and went to the door, not daring to hope it was her he'd find.

But it was.

Red-eyed, trembling. He pulled her into his arms.

13

MERCY ABANDONED HERSELF to Will, letting go of her reason and her doubts. If it was a mistake, so be it. This was probably the last chance she'd ever have to feel this way. She'd rather deal with whatever pain would come than live with constant regret.

"Mercy," he whispered, as he touched her hair, the small of her back. "I can't believe— Thank you, thank you."

She laughed, although she understood completely. If he hadn't been here, if he'd been sleeping, what would she have done? She kissed him, tasting the whiskey on his tongue, then tasting just Will.

He wore a robe and she slipped her hand inside the fold to find his chest wonderfully bare. "You were ready."

"Hopeful," he said. "But I thought—"

"I changed my mind."

His grin made her shiver. "Thank God."

Still keeping one hand inside his robe, she used the other to grab on to his belt to steer him toward the bedroom. "Is that basket still out?"

"I put it away."

"Then we have one stop to make."

She tried to make it the whole way without looking

behind her, but her aim was off by a tad. They finally made it to the armoire, where Will flung open the doors.

She looked inside at the array of toys and goodies, and her first thought was to try them all out, one after another until they collapsed, but then she thought about the other night, and how incredible it was to simply make love. She grabbed the condoms and shut the doors. "I want you," she said. "Just you."

"Then you have too many clothes on."

He pulled her toward the bed, then started fixing the problem. With nimble fingers he pulled off her T-shirt, and when she wrestled with her bra, he undid her jeans. Together, they made quick work of it, and then she was naked and his robe was on the floor.

He was already hard, and she slipped her hand around his erection, loving that she already knew how it felt. Not just in her hand, but inside her. She knew a lot about his body, but there was more to learn. She wanted a complete education.

His hands ran all the way down her back until he cupped her buttocks. Squeezing them once, he lifted her, and she wrapped her legs around him to keep her balance.

"I want everything," he said, "all at once."

"I know." She kissed him again, her hair obscuring his face, her thighs holding on tight.

He spun her around then lowered her to the bed. "Shit, I didn't pull down the covers."

"I don't care," she said, pulling him down with her.

He didn't miss a beat. His kiss was deep and long, and his hand cupped her breast. She couldn't get close enough to him, urgency making her heart pound as she touched him wherever she could.

He pulled back, locked on to her gaze. "Beautiful," he whispered.

She knew her eyes were swollen and red, that her skin was splotchy from crying, but she also knew he meant it. That to him, she was beautiful.

The lights were off, but the moon filled the room with a magic shimmer. She could see his face, read the desire in his eyes. "Make love to me," she said.

His slow smile was equal parts delight and passion. He slowed down, and she tried to do the same, finding a new rhythm by matching him breath for breath.

Her legs stretched out, spread for him, for whatever he wanted to do.

He lowered his mouth to her chin where he kissed her, nipped her, all the while stroking her body as if she were a cat. As if he could make her purr.

His slow hands stoked the fire that had never truly gone out since their first time. It astonished her that she could feel so alive, so sensitive. He'd found the key to her, the switch that changed her from the half-alive woman on the twentieth floor to this. Every inch of her vibrant, pulsing, needing.

She found his cock again, and she stroked him slowly. He shifted and she was able to cup his balls, to make him hiss as she rolled them gently with her fingers. Wanting more, she slid down his body, kissing his lightly haired chest, his hard little nipple, then his flat stomach. She followed the dark arrow down until her lips met her hand.

She licked him from the base to the crown, using the flat of her tongue, loving the sounds he made. Next, a warm breath following the moist path.

He tasted like sex, like man, like flesh, and though she'd never seen the appeal before, she did now. It was important, this taste. She needed to memorize him so when he was gone, she could conjure him in the lonely, dark nights.

No, she wouldn't think about that. Only now. Only this. Only here.

His hand moved to the back of her head and she froze, afraid. She couldn't stand it when they pushed her down. Pushed her until she couldn't breathe. But he didn't. He petted her. Caressed her. There was nothing forceful, only care.

She released her pent-up breath, then closed her eyes once more. This time, she put the crown in her mouth, letting the taste settle on her tongue before she swirled and teased and made him moan. Knowing he wouldn't hurt her, she let herself play. Not just with her mouth and her tongue, but with her teeth, her hand. It wasn't like anything she'd known before. Giving him pleasure gave her pleasure. Instead of doing a duty, a necessary evil, she found that she loved it. Each new sound he made, each time he stiffened and twitched, she felt a flush of pleasure in her own body. Another miracle. Another memory.

"Mercy, stop."

She did, pulling away quickly. "What's wrong? Did I hurt you?"

"God, no. It was amazing. A little too amazing, if you get my drift."

"Ah. Well, you know, we could always do it again."

"With you, I probably could. But I don't want to take the chance. I may only have the one shot, and I want it to count."

"It counts. Believe me."

"Not as much as it's going to," he said, sitting up, taking her by the shoulders and pulling her up to his kiss.

Somehow she was on her back, still deep in the throes of his kiss. His fingers were between her legs, stroking the outside of her pussy. This time, she did purr. She stretched and twisted and lifted her hips, thrusting herself onto him. She felt brazen, wild. This was it. Nothing in the world was going to stop her from doing everything she wanted.

"You're on fire," he whispered as he pushed two fingers deep. "Tight. Wet. And you're burning up."

"And that's just your fingers."

He moaned, dropping his forehead to her shoulder. "Careful. You're going to make me come without a touch."

"We wouldn't want that," she said. Then she spread her legs wide, a blatant invitation.

"Devil," he said. "Just for that, you wear the condom."

She laughed out loud. "It wouldn't do us much good, but if you hand one to me, I'll put it on you."

He rolled to the side of the bed and grabbed a packet. When he rolled back, he hesitated. "I'm not sure that's a good idea."

"Why? You think I don't know how? They're not very complicated."

"No. I'm afraid that if you touch me, I'm going to lose it."

"Chicken."

He clucked. Pretty convincingly. Then he put the condom on himself. He clucked once more, softly. In the moonlight, his dimples made her fall a little deeper.

"Come here, Chicken Little."

"Hey, watch it."

"Okay, Chicken Huge."

"Well, let's not get crazy."

She held him by the back of the neck and looked into his eyes. "I thought you were going to make love to me."

He got very serious, very fast. His fingers found her opening again and he thrust, hard. Then he clucked once more in a long, drawn-out refrain as he headed south.

THE SOUND OF HER laughter played in his head as he pulled out all the stops. She wouldn't be laughing for long. He opened her with his fingers, then he bowed his head. His tongue made her gasp, which was exactly what he wanted.

He didn't know why she'd come back to his bed, but he was going to make her remember every second of this. Not that it was a problem. She was a banquet, a feast of delight. No matter where he looked, what he touched or tasted, it was magic. There was no other way to explain it.

Maybe one. She'd made him crazy. That made more sense, actually. No way he should feel this way, not with her. Not like this. He wasn't supposed to know her, let alone care about her. She was a piece of the puzzle. That's all.

Drina could be stealing the collar right this second, and he didn't give one solitary damn. She could steal the crown jewels, and they couldn't get him out of this room with a crowbar.

Mercy had come back to him. She was here, in his bed. He hadn't felt this good in years.

She moaned, and his thoughts went up in smoke. His mouth and his cock took over and he was right there, centered, focused on one thing—making her come.

It didn't take long. He felt her muscles tighten, then a second later, she cried out, spasmed, squeezed his head between her thighs.

He had to struggle a bit to get free, to get himself in position, but she was still trembling when he thrust himself inside her.

He threw his head back in a blinding moment of utter pleasure. His eyes rolled back as his brain shorted out from the sheer intensity. No telling how long he was suspended in that bliss, but finally, he came back, and there was a whole new landscape of sensations to dive into.

She met his every thrust. Her breasts moved, her hands gripped the sheets, her stomach muscles clenched and he couldn't get enough, see enough. Mesmerized, he wanted it to go on and on forever.

But his cock had no patience whatsoever. Before he could do a thing about it, he felt the orgasm reach the point of no return. He grabbed her legs and put them on his shoulders. He lifted her up so he could go deep and hard. He stopped breathing as he went into her again and again until there was nothing in the universe except being inside Mercy and he came so hard he almost passed out.

An eon later, he gasped in a breath. His vision came back and he cursed that he'd been so crazy he hadn't watched her. He supposed it didn't matter, as she was so gorgeous now. Her hair wild and tangled, her lips parted, moist, and her eyes as dazed as he felt. Not to mention the way her chest heaved up and down as she tried to get her breath back. Now that was a sight.

DRINA HAD THEM in her sight, centered in the lens of the low-light camera.

It wasn't even that late, just before midnight, but they'd timed their break-in perfectly.

The two staff members watching the pets were in the back room, unloading supplies. The dogs were mostly sleeping, except for Pumpkin, of course. It didn't matter. Pumpkin barked incessantly.

The two of them were dressed for an evening out. Him in a tuxedo, her in a long black dress. They didn't so much as hesitate, once they were inside. But they did make enough noise for her to aim her camera.

She caught them walking straight back to the big cages, the ones they called suites. He opened the door to Lulu's room, and she went in. It didn't take but a moment. She came out, and thank God, Drina's camera caught the diamond collar in her hand. Then putting it in her pocketbook. He closed the door, and they walked out as quickly as they'd come.

Drina didn't stop filming until they had closed the door. She took the film cassette and put it in her pocket, just in case. One check to make sure she was alone, another fretful few moments to make sure the two of them had gotten in the elevator, then she, too, made her escape.

The hallway outside was empty. She walked slowly, as an old woman should, but inside she felt young again. *Marius, I have them now. I'm going to prove to all the world that they are scum. Watch, my darling, as I make them pay for the rest of their lives.*

"I WANT TO GET WATER," Will said. "But I don't think I can walk."

Mercy nodded. "Water sounds good. Maybe we should call room service."

"We'd have to pull up the covers."

"We can call room service, and tell them the waiter needs to wear a blindfold."

"Good one. You call."

Mercy was flat on her back, with Will sort of draped on top of her, at least on top of her left side. It didn't matter. She only had enough energy to keep on breathing. The talking thing would have to stop. She grunted.

"Yeah," he agreed.

Her eyes were closed, it was a little cold, except for where they touched, and she never wanted to move again. Screw leaving. Screw it if she got caught. She'd simply explain that it was the best sex anyone's ever had in the history of mankind. They'd understand. They'd be jealous, but they'd get it.

"Okay. I'm going," Will said. "See?"

He hadn't moved a muscle.

"It's okay. I don't mind dying of thirst. It was totally worth it."

He patted her hip, where his hand had landed. "Good girl."

"Just so you know? I'm not leaving. I hope it's okay, because, well, I'm not leaving."

"It's fine. Perfect. Excellent."

They got quiet again, the only sound the ever softer inhales and exhales.

"Mercy?"

"Huh?"

"I want you to stay. I mean that with every melted bone in my body. But I would shoot myself if you got in trouble over this."

She patted his ass. "Don't worry. If I get in trouble, I'll shoot you."

"Ah. Okay."

"Now go to sleep," she said.

"Can't."

"Why not?"

Surprising her, he sat up in flurry, then got to his feet. "I'll be back," he said as he headed to the bathroom.

She smiled. He was funny. She'd known he was funny, but he was funny in bed. That had to be the best thing ever. Okay, not *the* best thing, but close. She giggled, thinking of his clucks. Then she didn't giggle at all as she thought about what he'd done next.

By the time he came back carrying the water, she was actually feeling aroused again. She scooted up to let him arrange the covers, then drank a lot as he climbed back into bed.

He drank, then smiled at her. "Wow."

"I'll say."

"You're an animal."

She clucked. "So are you."

He dropped his head into his palm. "I'm not going to live that one down, am I?"

"I don't think so."

He looked at her again. "Ah, well."

"Speaking of clucking. How's the little rooster?"

His eyebrows shot up. "Seriously?"

She nodded, only a little guiltily.

"Tired, but not dead."

"Hmm. Let's see if we can wake him up."

HE WOKE UP TO FIND he was alone. A spear of disappointment shot through him, wondering when she'd left. How she'd left. If she would once again feel guilty or frightened. It had been the best night of his life. He'd hoped she'd felt the same.

He got out of bed and padded to the bathroom. There, on the counter, was a note. She'd written it at six-thirty this morning.

Dear Will. It's late. I have to go. I don't want to.

That was all. It was enough. He got into the shower, looking forward to seeing her face.

Forty-five minutes later, he walked into a madhouse.

His stomach sank. Drina had done it. He snuck past an officer guarding the door to see police crawling all over the place. The dogs were barking, the PetQuarters staff appeared traumatized. There was Piper Devon and who he assumed were other high-level staff, all of them looking seriously displeased.

But who he didn't see was the only one he cared about.

He went to Gilly, who was standing huddled next to Andrew. "What happened?"

"Someone stole Lulu's collar."

"Do they know who?"

Gilly looked as if she might start crying any second. "No. But they think it's one of us."

"No," he said, feeling the blood drain from his head.

"They've been all over Mercy. There are two detectives in her office. They've been in there for half an hour."

He turned to look at her closed door. They were going to pin this on Mercy. He couldn't let that happen. He had to get the collar back, make sure it was returned. And he'd have to give Mercy an alibi. An alibi that wouldn't get her fired.

But if push came to shove, and he had to choose between Mercy and his grandmother… "Shit," he whispered.

14

IT WAS ALMOST TIME for Drina to leave. She was tired. After all, she'd been awake the whole night. She'd broken into the Morrises' suite, into their safe. She'd filmed the contents: the collar, the insurance papers, the authentication that stated that the collar was made with real diamonds and was worth over a million dollars. It had gone exactly as she'd planned. How long had she waited for this? To catch the "Morrises" at their own game?

No one would have believed her without the proof. They would have dismissed her as old, senile, bitter. But she knew better.

The Morrises had created their life from nothing. Only fingerprints would tell the police that they were in truth the Cristescus. They would find a long list of arrests for petty larceny, for fraud. They wouldn't see what they'd done to Marius, but it wouldn't matter. Once she'd gotten all her proof, including a real authentication that would show the diamonds were all fake and that the insurance was fraudulent, the Cristescus would go to prison for the rest of their lives. Then Drina would be done. She would live out her days knowing she'd honored her husband.

But soon, she would go to the diamond district, to one of the most respected diamond men in the business.

She would record his statement, and include it with all the other evidence. Then she would go not only to the police, but to the *New York Times*. She would arrive with her package just after noon. The reporter would do some fact-checking, which she had made extraordinarily simple, and they would run the piece as an exclusive. That, she knew from a friend who worked for the *Times*.

It would all be over in a day or two. It probably wouldn't make the front page, but that was all right. The bastards would go to jail. They would pay.

She made sure she had everything she needed and headed out, wishing Will could have been her partner in this, instead of her enemy.

By FOUR-THIRTY, Will had searched Drina's room from top to bottom, but he hadn't found the collar. She must have put it in her safe, which meant he was going to have to talk her out of it.

If he hadn't been so wrapped up in Mercy last night, he could have avoided all of this. He should have been tailing Drina. The moment she stole the collar, he could have grabbed it before it went into the safe. Now he had to convince the stubborn old woman to hand it over to him. To help him save Mercy.

Not that it would be easy. Drina was on a mission, and better men than he had tried to swerve her off her course, only to be defeated. This time was different.

He needed to go check on Mercy. She'd still been with the police when he'd slipped away this morning. Once more, he rode to the twentieth floor, trying not to curse every stop along the way.

There was still a crowd in PetQuarters, and as it was now a crime scene, he had to explain to the police officer that his dog was inside. They'd made him sign a sheet after they checked his documents, but he'd finally gotten inside. It seemed as if the detectives had gone, but Mercy's office door was still closed. He searched until he found Gilly. "Is she still in there?"

"No. She left."

"What?"

"Honestly, I thought she was with you."

"Do they really think she did it?"

"No, I don't think so. But we're all suspects. We all have access. They searched all the lockers, and we've been questioned," Gilly said, but her voice cracked. Will saw she'd been crying, underscoring, as if he needed to be reminded, the urgency of the situation. "The thing is, she's totally taking the fall. She told them she was responsible. That no matter who actually took the collar, it was her fault." Gilly wiped her eyes with her fingertips, smearing her mascara.

"Why did she leave?"

"She resigned."

His whole body reacted. His anger at Drina was almost more than he could bear. He shook with rage, not just at his grandmother but at himself. "How long ago did she leave?"

"Maybe ten minutes ago."

"Thank you, Gilly."

"Go find her. She's so scared."

"I'll do my best." He moved, fast, to get back to the elevator and down to his floor. When he didn't see Mercy outside, his heart sank. He'd call her cell. He had no idea where she lived, but maybe Gilly did. Goddamn it, why had he gotten her into this? Why the hell had she resigned? It was all Drina's fault. His fault.

Cell phone in hand, he opened his suite door. There was Mercy, standing by the couch. She looked as if she'd been through a beating. She made a small sound as she headed toward him. He met her halfway, pulling her into his arms, and all he felt was guilt.

He'd been such an idiot. Of course Mercy had taken the blame. PetQuarters was her baby. She would be the first to stand up, to protect her employees. He'd been arrogant, thinking he could so easily outwit Drina. She was many things, none of them stupid. Of all the grifters he'd known, Drina was the queen. She'd hoodwinked more poor souls than he could count. Leaving her victims poorer, if not wiser.

Of all the people who didn't deserve to be Drina's mark, Mercy was on the top. But the tighter he held Mercy the clearer it was that he was the one responsible. He'd done this to Mercy. Ruined the best and only thing she had in her life.

"I should have been there last night," she said, her voice soft and shaky. "It's all my fault. I told them to keep the collar in the safe, but they wouldn't listen. I should have insisted. Told them we couldn't keep Lulu if they didn't safeguard the collar."

"You couldn't have known," he said, the lie burning a hole in his gut. "They'll find out who did this. I swear."

She held him tight, trembling in his arms. He'd never intended to hurt her. Never. But he'd been so cavalier with his lies.

Good God, he'd never given them a thought. For all

his derision, all his posturing about his family, he was just as bad. Worse. Because he pretended he had taken the high road.

He should tell her everything. Turn Drina into the police and let her deal with the fallout. Screw the promise to Marius. How could a promise to a dead thief matter when Mercy, of all people, was taking the blame?

But would turning in Drina take the pressure off Mercy? Or would her relationship with him brand her as an accomplice?

He wasn't going to take any more chances, not with so much at stake. He needed to find Drina, get the god-damned collar, and end this, now.

"Will?"

She'd said something. "I'm sorry, what?"

"I don't know what to do. I won't be able to get another job, not like this. That is, if I'm not in jail."

"You're not going to jail. I promise."

She looked up at him, and his heart shattered. "You can't be sure of that. I know it wasn't one of my people who did this. I know it. So someone from outside stole the collar. Someone they'll probably never find. That will leave me."

"That's ridiculous, Mercy. Anyone who's met you knows you couldn't have done it."

"You don't understand," she said, pulling away from him. She went to the couch and sat down.

"Tell me," he said as he sat next to her. He tried to take her hand, but she wouldn't let him.

"I was in trouble, when I was a kid. I kept running away. I got caught stealing some food when I was fourteen. One of the foster families accused me of robbing them, and I was put in juvie for three months. My record was never expunged." She sniffed and swiped her cheek with the back of her hand. "The only thing I've ever had was this job. Seriously. Before this, it was waitressing in dives or serving cocktails to horrible people. This job was beyond my wildest dreams, but when it all comes down to it, I'm the one with the record. Why should anyone believe me?"

He'd known she'd had a bad past, but she'd never told him the details. It made sense that she'd been in the system. That everyone in her life had lied to her, accused her, forgotten her. Wasn't it just what he'd done? Lied to get what he wanted? Planned on leaving her, after sleeping with her?

He never should have taken advantage of her last night. He'd known it wasn't good for her, but did he give a damn? All he'd cared about was his dick. The hell with Mercy. He couldn't even laugh at the bad pun, because it was too goddamn true.

"I should go home."

"You're tired. Why don't you go lie down?"

She shook her head. "I don't think I can."

He sighed. "Can you try? I'm going to find out what the police know, and check up on a few things myself."

"I don't want you getting involved."

He almost laughed. "Don't worry about it. Just rest. If you need anything, anything at all, you just call room service," he said. "Take what you want from the bar."

"I don't want anything. I don't know. I just don't think I can rest. I'll probably call Gilly, but I'll keep my cell on. Call me when you get back, okay?"

"The minute I return," he said. "And try not to worry. I swear, it will all be over soon. Everything's going to work out."

"That's sweet. But you can't know. I'm an easy target," she said. "No one will blink when it all ends up on my lap."

He pulled her up and hugged her. "It won't. I give you my word." As if that meant anything.

She turned to kiss him. He didn't want to. She shouldn't ever have to kiss a man like him. But he did. It tasted like shame.

WILLIAM WAS WAITING in the lobby when Drina made it back to the hotel. She frowned as she headed toward the elevator. Things hadn't gone so smoothly today. The collar was still with the diamond expert. She wouldn't be able to reclaim it until tomorrow. Unfortunately, the reporter she was supposed to meet wouldn't be there tomorrow. She'd have to find someone else if she didn't want to wait. But then, what difference would two days make?

Of course, William caught up to her halfway through the lobby. "Drina, where's the collar?" he whispered as he took hold of her arm.

She spun on her grandson. "Go away. This isn't your business."

"I can't let this happen."

"I'm not afraid to get you in trouble, William. I can scream, right now. You know I can and that they'll believe me."

"I know you can. I'm hoping you won't."

"Why should I do anything for you?"

He paused as a young woman walked by. As soon as

she was out of earshot, he was at it again. "Because I don't want to go to the police."

"The police? You think they'll find anything? Surely you haven't forgotten everything your grandfather taught you. Never leave a trail, William. It's the first lesson."

"Just sit down with me, would you? There's an innocent person getting crucified for this. We can work something out."

Drina jerked her arm out of his grasp. Her arm would have bruises tomorrow, but did he care? "Your little friend will be proven innocent. She won't go to jail or lose her job. Just go back and comfort her. Use her some more, until she embarrasses you and you leave her behind."

"I'll admit, I have nothing but regrets about how I treated Mercy. I lied to her just the way I'd been taught. Now her life is falling apart. I'm not proud of it."

"But you're willing to throw your own grandmother to the wolves? There's something to be proud of. I'm nothing to you. A reminder of all you despise. Never mind that it was your grandfather who made sure you went to your fancy college. That it was your family who kept you from living on the street."

"And I appreciate all that. I just wanted a different life."

"So you couldn't be different and respect your elders? You had to spit on us to shine your shoes? What kind of a grandchild is that?"

"A terrible one."

Drina laughed at the repentance on his face. It was just as false as his name. She leaned closer to him. "You can't con me," she said. "I know more about the game than you ever will."

"I'm not trying to con you. I wouldn't dare. But if

you would just talk to me, maybe there's a way we can both get what we want."

"But William, I don't care what you want. I'm an old woman, and I've lived through more disappointments than you could count. There are two that tore my soul. Marius being betrayed. And you. I can do something about the first one. You, I've given up on. You can go be with your fancy friends at your operas and galas and your dinner parties. If you go to the police, I swear to you, it will only make things worse."

"You won't spend five minutes?"

She looked at him, at what a fine-looking man he'd become. But after all this time, after all he'd shown her was disrespect and contempt, she felt nothing. That in itself was a sin, but it was too late. She turned from him.

"Drina, don't do this."

With her back straight and Marius close to her heart, she said, "It's already done. You can rest easy that you played your part." Then she walked away.

MERCY STOOD FROZEN behind the pillar in the lobby. Her whole body trembled and she felt so weak she had to hold on to the cold marble just so she wouldn't fall.

When Gilly hadn't answered her phone, Mercy had decided to go for a walk. She just had to get out of the hotel, even if she couldn't bear to go home. Of course, she'd left Will a note, but then she'd seen him as she got off the elevator.

She'd almost caught up to him when he'd stopped the woman. Drina Dalakis. Pumpkin's mother. The moment she saw him grab her arm, Mercy's heart had fallen and her world had tilted on its axis.

Something made her move behind the pillar. While she hadn't heard everything she'd heard enough. Mrs. Dalakis was Will's grandmother. Mercy remembered clearly the day the two of them had been together at Pet-Quarters. Will had acted as if she didn't know her. They'd both pretended. Lied.

Mercy wasn't sure how, but she understood that together, they'd stolen the dog collar.

Everything Will had told her was a lie. Everything he'd done to her was a lie. Everything she'd come to love about him was a lie.

He was a thief. And he'd used her in every way possible. He'd known from the start that she would be blamed. That she would lose everything. And still, he'd made her love him.

Her stomach heaved and she covered her mouth and ran to the nearest bathroom, barely making it into the stall. She was as sick as she'd ever been, as if she'd been poisoned, which she had.

When the spasms stopped, she slid down to the cold marble floor. It occurred to her that she wasn't crying. Shouldn't she be crying?

For a supposedly street-smart kid like her, she'd been the perfect dupe. She'd bought his line completely. Given herself to him like a Christmas present, all wrapped up in a nice bow.

It had been the most exciting, wonderful experience of her life, and it was all bullshit. Nothing. Fake.

She deserved to lose her job. To lose everything.

15

WILL HAD STARED after Drina long enough. He wasn't going to change her mind. The woman was the definition of stubborn. Even if he explained who Mercy was and what she'd come to mean to him, Drina wouldn't care. Why should she?

He headed for the bar. He needed to figure this damn thing out, come up with a way to save both Mercy and Drina. What he needed was a miracle, even though he was the last person on earth who deserved one.

The bar was crowded and noisy, but he managed to find a seat that was almost against the back wall. He ordered a scotch—a double—and stared at nothing until it arrived.

Drina had to know that fencing the collar was going to be discovered. He'd seen reporters in PetQuarters along with the police. The story would be in the papers by tonight's evening edition. Jesus, this was the kind of story the *Post* would jump all over. Who knows what they were going to say about Mercy?

His thoughts skipped and lurched, finally sticking on the Morrises—the owners of the collar. Were they part of this mess? Why had they insisted on Lulu wearing the damn collar? Anyone with a lick of sense would have put the damn thing in a safe, at the very least when Lulu was inside the pet hotel.

He could chalk it up to stupidity, but it was rare to find truly rich stupid people, if they hadn't inherited the money, that is. According to his research, Morris had made his fortune. So why had they been so bullheaded about the diamonds?

And, he wondered yet again, why was Drina so hell-bent on stealing the damn thing? She didn't have the kind of wealth that would buy penthouses and yachts, but she was well off. Marius had always squirreled away cash, enough for any emergency, and Drina bought what she wanted.

Come to think of it, that might have changed in recent years. How would he know? He avoided her whenever possible. She might have had some heavy expenses, and this was her way of refilling the coffers.

If it was, then he was to blame for that, too. Drina, no matter what, was his grandmother. He should have been watching out for her, and not because of some deathbed promise. What kind of a man had he become?

If it wasn't so real, so horrifying, he would have laughed. His house of cards had crumbled around him in the blink of an eye.

He stared at his empty glass, wishing he had the whole bottle. He had to make things right. Sadly, he had no idea how.

MERCY STARED OUT the window of the bus, not seeing a thing. She had her backpack in her arms, but there was no comfort to be found. There was no comfort in the world that could help her.

Even when she tried to stop, memories of Will kept bombarding her like darts. The sweeter the memory, the sharper the point.

It shouldn't have shocked her. Not really. Her life had been one giant lesson in disappointment. Having to resign from her job at PetQuarters? Of course. What else should she expect. The only times she'd ever gotten anything good, it had been taken away.

That first time she'd been sent to a foster family, she'd been excited. She'd dreamed, back then, of being adopted. It would be just like the movies. They'd have their adjustments to make, but she'd learn to trust her new guardians, and someday, they would love each other.

It had taken a whole four days for that dream to shatter. The first time good ol' Greg had crawled into her twin bed for "special time" was all she'd needed to know.

Still, that hadn't been enough of a lesson. From the age of five to seventeen, she'd gone through seven foster families. By number six, she'd begged to be left alone. She'd run away, only to be dragged back.

The one thing that had saved her, that had made it important not to dive into drugs or just end it, was animals. Dogs, mostly, but it didn't matter what kind. She loved them all. Especially the ones like her, who'd been kicked around, abandoned.

She would go back to the animal shelter. If they'd have her. If she wasn't in jail. But she'd been okay at the shelter. It had been so simple. And they'd let her hang out as long as she wanted. No diamond dog collars to worry about. No quotas, no big ideas about spoiled pets. She'd go back to being a waitress. She'd survived that, she could do it again. As for living in the pit? She could take it. There was no choice.

Her throat tightened and fresh tears burned her eyes. She wiped them away furiously, cursing Will Desmond with every vile word she knew.

Why did he have to make it so personal? What did sleeping with her get him? He could have gotten everything he wanted by just hanging out at PetQuarters, so why? Did he get his kicks making women love him, only to laugh as they died inside? Was that the real prize?

She kept thinking about that day she'd seen him with Mrs. Dalakis and they'd pretended to be strangers. She'd never heard of a grandmother/grandson team, but why not? At least they kept it all in the family.

God, she'd actually fantasized about marrying him. Her, of all people. The story in her head had warmed her like a blanket. She'd even figured out how many dogs and cats they'd have. And their names.

Pathetic. She'd forgotten everything life had taught her. But this would be the last time. No one was getting inside again. Ever. All she had to do was think of him, and it would be a piece of cake.

IF WILL HADN'T BEEN convinced already that Mercy lived in a bad neighborhood, he got it now. He paid the cabby and got out. Music assailed him, although it was difficult to call it that. The bass was so loud it vibrated inside him like an earthquake. The sound alone would have been enough to drive him away, but there was a group of gang-bangers hanging out on a front stoop who looked as if they would kill him just for something to liven up the night.

Luckily it wasn't Mercy's stoop. He hurried up her steps and inside, the dim lights and unsavory smells making him want to pull her out of here so she never again had to face this horror.

He climbed the stairs and knocked on the door, dreading what he would see inside. Not just the state of the apartment, but Mercy. Her note had seemed desperate. He wasn't at all sure how he could make her feel better, especially now that he'd failed so miserably with Drina.

The door swung open to reveal not Mercy, but a tall, skinny kid with long, stringy black hair and no shirt, but enough tattoos to make Will take a step back. The boy, maybe seventeen, was covered with them, from his wrists to his neck to the edge of his very low-hanging jeans.

"Yeah?"

"Is Mercy here?"

The boy shrugged as he stepped back, revealing a nightmare space. Three ratty couches, an old beat-up TV on a couple of apple crates, clothes littering the stained carpet. It looked like a crack den and smelled like stale cigarettes and pot.

"Back there." The kid pointed to a closed door on the right.

Picking his way over things that made his skin crawl, he got to Mercy's door and knocked.

A minute or two went by, and just as he'd decided to try the knob, the door swung open. Her face registered shock. But then, an instant later, that shock turned into such a look of hatred it made him gasp. "What's wrong?"

"Get out," she said.

"What?"

She swung the door at him, but he caught it with his shoulder. Mercy turned around and went to the edge of a small bed in what had to be the tiniest bedroom in the city.

"Mercy, what's going on?"

"I don't want you here. Go away."

"Honey, talk to me."

"Honey?" she repeated. "That's just perfect. Well, bad news for you. I know. I'm on to you and your grandmother. I get it."

Will's heart sank like a stone. "No, you—"

"I heard you," she said, her voice a hell of a lot louder and infinitely more angry. "I was in the fucking lobby. I heard you. I know you two planned the robbery, and I know you planned on me taking the fall. Okay. Fine. Great job, both of you. You pulled it off without a hitch. Now get the hell out of my house."

He tried to remember everything he'd said to Drina. It hadn't seemed damning at the time, but the exact words were already gone. "Let me explain."

"Explain what? How you decided it would be extra giggles if you could get me to sleep with you? And major laughs if the stupid street kid fell in love? Yeah, I got all that."

"No. That's not how it was."

"What in hell makes you think I'm going to believe one word out of your lying mouth?"

"Nothing. There's no reason. But please, just know that I never meant you to get hurt. You were never supposed to be involved in this."

"Oh, please. I know you can do better than that. What, did you steal Buster from some backyard?

Maybe you discarded a few puppies before you found Buster 'cause they weren't cute enough? Interesting that granny chose Pumpkin though. A barker, that was pretty smart. I knew something was wrong there. Pumpkin never trusted her, and I was too stupid to listen to the only thing that might have warned me."

"It wasn't like that. I was at Hush to stop Drina. I knew she was going to do something foolish, but I didn't know what until I found out she'd bought a dog. That led me to PetQuarters. I had to find out what she was up to, and stop her before it got too serious."

"Really? Did you tell her you were going to rat her out the first chance you got? Or is that just the way the game is played?"

"She didn't know I was there for several days. I was watching her. Making sure she didn't get herself into trouble."

Mercy picked up a book and threw it against the wall. A bookmark covered with dog pictures landed on her comforter. "I don't want to hear this. I just want you to go."

"I'll finish, and then if you still want me to—"

"I will. I do."

"I figured out she was going to steal the collar. I'm still not sure why, but I know her well enough to recognize when she's on a mission. I was supposed to be keeping a close watch on her. When she stole the collar, I was going to steal it right back, make sure it was around Lulu's neck. No one would have been the wiser."

"Stop it. You can't even speak without lying."

"The reason I wasn't there, wasn't watching her, was because all I could think of was you."

Mercy laughed, but the sound made him sick. He'd

messed this up so badly. He should just turn around and walk out. Nothing he could say would make the situation better. She'd never believe him and she shouldn't. He'd treated her unspeakably badly.

"You're right. I never should have gotten close to you. I never intended to like you so much. It just happened."

"It's over now. You can rest easy that you've played your part."

"I can't. I'm not going to let this fall on you."

She didn't even say anything. But the look she gave him—hurt, scared, unbelievably sad—cut to the core.

"She's a con artist, I'll give you that." Will raked a hand through her hair. "So was my grandfather and my parents. My whole damn extended family are grifters, always have been. I was raised to be one, too. My parents both died in prison. Drina's husband died there, too. My brother is dead, my sister is in a cult, where I'm positive she's stealing everyone blind. Only my grandfather, he made me promise him that Drina wouldn't end up in prison. Despite what he'd done, who he was, I still cared about him. I used to visit him in jail. I swore to him that I'd keep her safe. She hasn't made it easy."

"I swear to God, if you don't leave here right now I'm calling the police."

"It's true. I know I shouldn't have lied to you. It doesn't matter that I was trained to lie from the first moment I could speak. I should have come up with another way. The truth is, it never occurred to me not to lie. There I was holding myself so far above them. Thinking they were crap because of how they lived, and I was just as bad. I lied the way some people breathed.

It was easier, that's all. And I never stuck around to see any fallout."

Mercy reached down the bed and pulled her backpack to her lap. She opened it, finding her cell phone on top. "I'm calling the police. I'm not afraid of a little lying myself. Then it will be your turn to be questioned by the police."

"All right. I'm going. But I still won't let you take the rap. I swear. Mercy, I'm sorry."

She put her finger on the keypad, and he turned around. It made him sick to leave her in this squalid hell. But that was nothing compared to the hell he'd put her through.

Mercy was one of the best things to ever happen to him. Even in the short time he'd known her, he'd felt better, looked forward to his days, laughed more. She was special. Clearly far more special than he deserved.

There was only one thing left to do. In fact, it was Mercy's words that helped him see exactly what came next.

He made it to the street without getting stabbed or shot. But then he had to wait for a cab. It was altogether one of the most unpleasant experiences of his life.

She was up there, hating him. He'd done it to himself, and he deserved it. But he'd seen her pain. She didn't deserve that. Not by a long shot.

Damn him to hell.

DRINA HAD DONE all she could. The diamond man had called. He'd seen the fakery instantly, and had agreed to let her tape him as he discussed his findings. First thing tomorrow, she would collect everything she needed and she'd turn it all over to the police and the newspaper.

She looked down at the large envelopes sitting next to her on her hotel bed. Large enough to include video-tapes, insurance documents, everything. Enough evidence for any court in the land. The bastard betrayers would go to jail and rot there.

She had brought an address label with her. It was pure sentiment, but she'd written the address almost two years ago, when she'd realized not only that the bastards were planning an incredible con, but also, more importantly, that it had been the two of them, husband and wife, second cousins, who had betrayed him. Stolen from him. Put him in prison.

She knew at that moment she would do whatever it would take to exact her revenge. She wondered what she was going to do to fill her days from now on, but she didn't care. As far as she was concerned, it would be a good time for God to take her. There was no one left for her. Yes, she had friends, but playing cards was nothing to stay alive for. She missed her Marius.

She missed her son, her daughter, her grandchildren. She missed so much of her old life. It was past her time. She could feel Marius calling.

It was late and she was tired. Tonight she would dream of her victory, and shut out all thoughts of her grandson. In many ways, his betrayal was the hardest to swallow. How she'd loved him. His quick mind, how he'd loved to come over all by himself to have dinner with her and Marius.

She picked up the remote and aimed it at the television, but there on the news was the Hush lobby. She watched, anxious to see what they said about the theft.

The newscaster's words made her throat close. An arrest had been made. But how? She hadn't turned over the evidence yet.

Then she saw it. Him. His hands behind his back, he was walking between two policemen. William.

"William Desmond, CEO of WD Fitness Equipment of New York, confessed to stealing the diamond dog collar belonging to Mr. and Mrs. George Morris."

Drina watched the screen, barely hearing the rest of the story. She remembered the last time she'd seen someone she loved beyond measure go off that way. It wasn't right. She'd told him everything would turn out for his little friend.

It hadn't occurred to her that William could be in love. He'd never been in love, and she'd assumed he never would be.

"Damn fool," she whispered, as he was led to the front door.

It served him right. He had behaved despicably. He'd hurt her as deeply as she'd ever been hurt. She turned off the television and the light by her bed. She didn't dream of her victory, however. She barely slept. Because, despite everything, she still loved him.

"So you're saying you just lost the collar."

Will was in an interrogation room at the midtown precinct. There was a metal table between him and his interrogators, a microphone in front of him, cameras recording everything and a smell of desperation that clung to each breath. The detectives looked as bored as he felt.

It had been a good two hours since he'd turned himself in, but they kept asking him the same questions.

He thought about calling in an attorney, just so he could get a break. He was thirsty, tired, heartsick. But there had been no choice.

If Drina had been telling the truth, then he would be out of here in a few days. If she wasn't… The important thing was that all the suspicion would be off Mercy. She'd have her job back, safe and sound.

He honestly didn't care, except for the prospect of being held in such a dangerous place as Rikers Island. Although at this point, so what? He'd already been stabbed in the back, which wasn't an easy thing to do to oneself.

"Where did you take it after you got it from the dog?" This from the tall, thin detective with the ink spot on his breast pocket. Will figured he'd recently lost weight because his collar and his cuffs seemed too loose.

"Outside. I must have dropped it on the street."

"Dropped it on the street," the second detective muttered. "Look, Mr. Desmond, it's not possible a man as successful as you could be that stupid. Stealing the diamonds, all right. That at least makes some sense. But to expect us to believe you stole it, then dropped it on Madison Avenue? Come on."

Will sighed. This detective was shorter, rounder and had a surprisingly thick Southern accent.

"I know it sounds bad. But that's the deal."

"How did you get into PetQuarters, anyway?"

Now here was a story they would believe. One he knew all too well. "I was raised to be a grifter. Getting in locked doors, turning off alarms, taking what's not mine, that's nothing. I've been doing that since I was five years old."

Of course he hadn't mentioned lying. Perhaps his greatest skill of all.

_16_

MERCY HATED SITTING in the so-called living room. It smelled horrible and she always felt she needed a shower after sitting down. But when Toby had told her the guy who had been to see her was on the morning news, she'd felt compelled to watch.

Now she was more confused than ever. She knew Will hadn't taken the collar. Yes, he'd certainly been an accomplice, but from what the reporter was saying, he claimed to have taken the collar, acted alone, then proceeded to lose the collar.

It was a ridiculous story. No one was going to believe him. Even the reporter questioned Will's losing the collar on the street. She knew Will could do better. He was a master at lying. He could have spun a completely convincing tale without missing a beat. So what the hell was he doing?

She heard her cell phone ring and went to her bedroom to fetch it. It was Gilly. Mercy answered.

"What the hell is going on?" Gilly asked.

"Gilly, I just can't—"

"Did you know he was going to turn himself in?"

"No," Mercy said, wanting to beg off the conversation, but she needed Gilly. It was hard to admit, but it was true. Mercy couldn't see straight, not after all that had happened. Not after her horrible sleepless night. After crying until she had no more tears. If by some miracle she was offered her job back, she was for sure going to need someone to lean on.

"He didn't do it though. He was with you."

"What?"

"Mercy, come on. I know he was with you the night of the burglary. He couldn't have stolen the collar."

Tears welled up and she didn't even try to blink them away. "It's complicated."

Gilly sighed. "Tell me."

"You don't want to—"

"Mercy. Please. Tell me. I need to understand this."

Debating the wisdom of spilling her guts, in the end, Mercy was just too worn-out to come up with a good reason to put off her friend. She climbed under her comforter, grabbed a handful of tissues and wept with fresh tears as she spilled her heart out. Everything from the police questioning her to her resignation. Even the way Will had comforted her. When she got to the part where she overheard Will and his grandmother/accomplice, Gilly kept saying, "What?" and "You've *got* to be kidding me."

It took Mercy all the tissues she'd grabbed plus the rest of the box to get to the bitter end.

"Well, crap. This doesn't make sense at all."

"Except for the part where I'm a moron."

"Actually, that's the part that makes the least sense."

"Uh, thanks?"

"You know what I mean. First of all, I was there when Will confessed. He didn't say squat about an accomplice. In fact, he made sure everyone knew he acted alone."

"He's got something up his sleeve, Gilly. You have to see that."

"Just wait. I'm thinking. Why would he confess to something he didn't do?"

"Because he's guilty."

"Aside from being a jackass though, from what you said, he wasn't trying to get the collar so much as put the collar back."

"Gilly, this is ridiculous. The man lied to me about everything."

"Yeah. That part doesn't make sense, either."

"The only thing that bewilders me is why. I mean, he could have gotten everything he wanted without putting me in the middle. He didn't seem like a sociopath. I mean, the dogs all liked him, and you know how dogs are."

"Screw the dogs, and you know I don't mean that, but here's the point. While you put your faith in people-reading dogs, I put my faith in people-reading you."

"What?"

"Of everyone I know in the world, I trust your instincts the best. I know you won't believe me because you're also fabulous at not seeing the truth about yourself, but dude, it's true. If someone doesn't pass the Mercy test, that's it. No questions asked. Why do you think I told you to go for it with Will?"

"Because you're as dumb as me?"

"Because you already liked him. You let him walk the dogs. That's huge. And excuse me, but doesn't it keep coming up about how the employees at PetQuarters have the best employee records of any department in the hotel?"

"And that has to do with Will...?"

"You interviewed each one. And you were right, one hundred percent."

"It never crossed my mind that he was lying. Not once. I have no idea about this man. I don't even know if Will Desmond is his real name."

"I'm not trying to justify that part. I swear. But that's not all of it."

"It's all that matters."

"I don't think so, sweetie. He didn't know he was going to fall in love with you. He just knew his crazy grandma was going to do something monumentally stupid. He did what he did to protect her."

"That's convenient, but I'm not buying it."

There was a long silence, but finally, Gilly sighed again before she said, "I don't mean this to be unthinking, but I gotta say it. Honey, you don't have a grandma. You've never had someone you loved who made you insane. I'm sorry, but it's true."

"And you have?"

"Yep. I have."

"Would you have done what Will did to protect his grandmother?"

"Maybe not exactly, but I would have gone real far. Jail far."

"I don't know, Gilly. You may be completely right. It's just not enough."

"Okay. I get that. Lying is a big super-honkin' huge deal. It's just that, you know, I would have jumped Will's bones on day one, just because he's gorgeous. But you? He's the first guy you've liked in years. It didn't matter that he was too stunning for this planet. You and your dogs saw something else. Something good. And that's all I'm gonna say, except why don't you come back here? It's too depressing staying at your place and I swear, I'll keep everyone out of your hair."

"I don't work there anymore."

"Mercy, no one thinks you stole anything."

"It was my responsibility. Nothing can change that."

"What, you think every time someone puts a robe in their suitcase, Janice Foster resigns? It's a hotel, sweetie. Lots of people. Lots of bad people. You told the Morrises to put the damn collar in a safe. They refused. End of your responsibility."

"That's nice, but—"

"It's not nice. It's true. Your job is safe. You're not to blame. There's no reason in the world you should have to be trapped in that hovel of yours, especially with all that's going on. Please. Come back. PetQuarters isn't even closed off anymore. The police finished yesterday. We need you. The dogs need you."

Mercy sniffed. "I'll think about it," she said. Not just about her job, but about Will. She knew Gilly pretty damn well, and the fact that she was sticking up for him didn't make a whole lot of sense.

"You have a visitor."

Will stood, hoping like hell it was Mercy, although he wasn't at all sure what he would say to her. Turning himself in was the only thing he could have done, but now that the police had stopped questioning him, all he'd done was obsess over what an idiot he'd been and pepper himself with thoughts of how his confession was going to damage his business and his reputation.

After a sleepless, horrible night, he was still in his

small cell at the midtown precinct, but he expected to be taken to Rikers Island any minute. He really should call an attorney. If nothing else, the trip to the prison might be delayed.

He was taken from the cell, cuffed, then walked down a long hallway until they reached a metal door. No one was there. Just a table and two chairs, and a great big two-way mirror. It was hell to be cuffed again, this time to the metal chair, but if that brought Mercy closer...

It was Drina. She was dressed in the regal garb she favored, this time all white with green jewelry. She looked like a Fifth Avenue doyenne, and that's just how the guard treated her.

"Drina," he said.

She sat down and put her manicured hands on the ugly table. For a long time, she just stared at him, her eyes the same vivid blue he remembered from child-hood. Just older. Infinitely sadder. "What have you done, William?"

"What I had to," he said, keeping his voice down. He wasn't sure who was listening in, just knew that someone was.

"But you didn't. I told you. Things are in motion. All will come clear soon."

"*Soon* is longer than I could let Mercy be a suspect."

"Even if she did resign from her job, she'll be rein-stated. There will be no permanent damage."

He smiled at her. In so many ways she was still the grandma of his youth. Instead of fairy tales, he'd been told bedtime stories about con games, about hopeless saps who deserved what they got. Collateral damage was never discussed, never acknowledged. So what that it was a life savings they'd stolen? A college fund? When he'd asked, "what about the victim," he'd been scolded, as if he should know better.

"You do realize I can see your contempt."

Will inhaled sharply. What the hell was the matter with him? Was his better-than-thou attitude so ingrained that he couldn't go five minutes without mocking Drina? She was a product of her environment, of her parents and their parents. If she hadn't changed in sixty-four years she wasn't going to change. Period. That left him with only a few choices. Walk away and feel superior, or accept her for who she was. But then he'd already made his choice, just not very gracefully, it turned out. "I'm sorry. I have a tendency to do that, but I'm trying to stop."

She wasn't buying it. "You're not a stupid man, William. What is it about this girl?"

"I'm not just doing this for Mercy. I'm doing it for you."

"Do not say that. I don't need your help, I haven't ever needed your help. Whatever you promised Marius, I release you. You're no longer bound, do you understand?"

"I didn't do this because of Marius. The idea of something happening to you was untenable."

"What?"

"Despite my being a jerk about almost everything, I love you. I hadn't let myself believe that, but it's true. I was so concerned with not carrying on the legacy that I forgot the bottom-line truth. You're my grandma. I love you. I don't want anything bad to happen to you."

"But you disapprove of everything I am."

He nodded. "That's another thing I'll be working on. I can only decide what's right for me. That's all. I have no business judging you."

"This is all lovely talk, but you haven't answered my question. What is it about this girl?"

"I'm pretty sure I'm in love with her. And very sure I've blown any chance of having her." He tried to lean forward but was held back by the handcuffs. "I lied to her, Drina. Without a moment's hesitation. I lied to her even as I became involved with her. The funny thing was, until she caught me, until I saw the look of disgust and betrayal in her face, I didn't even know. I hadn't given it a minute's thought.

"I've been so busy feeling superior and self-righteous I never even bothered to stop and look at my own behavior."

"Be contrite, William, if you must. Just don't take it too far. Martyr is not a good look for you. Get out of here. It will all be over before you know it."

"I want to believe you, Drina."

She gave him a small, wry smile. "One thing I've never done is lie to my family. You hear me?" She reached into her pocketbook and took out a business card. "Call him. He'll take care of everything."

Will looked at the card, then back at Drina, who'd stood. If he could have, he would have taken her in his arms. He still didn't approve of her old ways, but who cared? Drina didn't need his approval. Will needed hers.

MERCY HAD GONE TO PetQuarters, doing her best not to catch anyone's eye as she went through the hotel. Gilly had been right about one thing, at least. There was no comfort in the place she had to call home. At least at Hush she could be with the animals, and really, there was no place else she'd rather be.

Gilly found her the moment she walked inside. Her friend pulled Mercy into a big hug, and she didn't let go for a long time. That Mercy cried again was not a shock. Since she first discovered the robbery she'd been riding a tiger, holding on for dear life. How could so much change in such a short period of time?

"I'm so glad you came," Gilly said, pulling her toward the little-dog pen. "I know it's early, but I've already made up our beds. And I've taken care of lunch, and I don't give a damn if you tell me you're not eating, because I know you haven't eaten squat and you need to."

Mercy couldn't help but smile. Leave it to Gilly, the great mother hen.

A bunch of the gang were there, including Eddy and Chrissy, who should have had the day off, and whoa, there were at least four of the interns who weren't on the schedule. It seemed as if they were all holding a dog, or getting a dog, which was weird.

She sat down and was immediately attacked by Buster, the Kid, Chance and Pumpkin, who was barking up a storm. Then Rosie was there, and Snickers and Jessie. They weren't supposed to be in with the little dogs, but she didn't care. The pups were scrambling all over her until she was just plain covered in dog. She petted anything that came in reach, and they licked and grinned, and yes, barked, as they rolled around and loved each other.

Her pet therapy lasted a lot longer than it should have, but she was in no mood to discipline anyone.

There were no growls, though, and not a hint of aggression, so who cared.

It made her feel better and it stopped her from thinking about him.

"Okay, you rangy mutts," Gilly yelled. "Enough!"

One by one, the dogs were taken. Soon, it was just her, Buster and Pumpkin. As she got herself in a sitting position and tried to wipe some of the slobber off her face, the two little dogs did something they'd never done before. They started playing. Together. No barking, no growling. Buster had always been willing, but Pumpkin would have nothing to do with him.

Until today.

"That's weird."

Mercy looked up to find Gilly watching the spectacle. "I'll say. Hey, I have a wild idea."

"What's that?"

"Let's get some lunch in you, and then you go get some sleep. You look like hell."

"Thanks so much."

Gilly held out her hand. "Come on. You have to be exhausted. Nothing's going to happen in the next hour and if it does, I swear I'll wake you."

Mercy doubted she would sleep, but it was true she needed something to eat. She took Gilly's hand and stood. "Thanks."

Gilly just grinned.

She fell asleep as soon as her head hit the pillow. What seemed like just five minutes later, Gilly's hand was on her shoulder, gently shaking her awake. "What happened?"

"It's almost dinner. And there's someone here."

"Dinner?" Mercy sat up, confused and still woozy with sleep.

"We're closing up. I just thought I'd give you a chance to, you know, brush your teeth or something."

Mercy yawned. "Did you say someone's here?"

"Take your time. She's not going anywhere." With that, Gilly walked away.

Mercy stared at the door as she struggled to wake, but then it all came back to her. All the lies. All the pain. She forced herself up and into the bathroom. Cool water on her face did nothing to ease her puffy, red eyes. She looked terrible, felt worse. Not sure why she bothered, she ran a brush through her hair and donned a clean Hush jacket.

She walked into the main room and looked for Gilly. When she found her, Mercy stopped cold. Next to Gilly was Drina Dalakis. She didn't look like a lying thief. In fact, she looked just like Pumpkin's owner, the rich woman who didn't know how to handle a dog. Maybe that's because the dog was just a prop. Just like Mercy herself. A prop. Someone to discard the moment the job was finished.

The woman walked over to her, and Mercy forced herself to stand her ground when she desperately wanted to run.

"I know you don't want to talk to me. That seems quite logical and fair. But I would ask that you give me a few moments of your time."

"Why should I do that?"

"Because my grandson is in jail for you, and I would like to see him get out of there before something happens that can't be taken back."

It was tempting to throw the thief out on her tail. Or to have Gilly tape her confession just before calling the police. "How can I believe anything you have to say?"

"You can believe or not believe. That's up to you."

Mercy headed toward her office, knowing Mrs. Dalakis would follow her, and she supposed she had nothing to lose by letting her. All she cared about was not making a fool of herself. Not bursting into tears. She needed to have one win in this whole mess. Just one.

When they sat down, Mercy tried to will her heart to slow, but it was hearing none of that.

"William was raised a thief," Mrs. Dalakis said without preamble. "I know this, because I raised him. He was taught that a lie was always better than the truth. It was part of his very religion to find other's weaknesses. To exploit what he found.

"But William turned his back on that life. He went to college. He went into business. Legitimate business. He owns a successful company that he built from nothing. He has turned his back on everything he was taught as a child. He lost his parents, his brother. The only reason he was here was to try and stop me from doing what he thought was dangerous and foolish."

"He told me. It doesn't make any difference. He lied to me about everything."

The woman put her hands on the desk. She seemed much older up close. Or maybe that was her guilt, eating at her. "He loves you."

"He has a hell of a way of showing me."

"You don't know how strong he is. He's very special. And he's very sorry. For what it's worth, I think you've given him the wake-up call of a lifetime. I doubt very much he will make the same mistakes twice."

Mercy shook her head. "We all have stories. I've got a story. It doesn't mean I get to steal and lie."

"You're right. It doesn't. So hate me. Blame me. I don't mind. I'm doing what I need to do. But listen to William. He's in jail for you. Do you understand? He's in jail for me, despite everything I stand for. He did things poorly. That's true. But to have him do this thing, isn't that the kind of man you want at your side?"

"Did he send you?"

"No."

"Does he know how he's going to get himself out of jail?"

"At the very longest, he'll only be held another day. This is also why I came to see you. I want to tell you why I did what I did. May I?"

Whether it was stupid or not, Mercy nodded. And listened.

17

EXHAUSTED AND DEFEATED, Will entered his suite at Hush at a quarter to three in the morning. Drina's lawyer had pulled God knows what strings to get him bail just before ten last night. It had taken until two-thirty for him to actually walk out the door.

The stay had been a short one, but sobering nonetheless. Not that he was sorry. He'd do it again tomorrow if it meant that Mercy would be okay.

Now, though, he desperately needed a shower. He stripped in the bathroom, and the luxury and freedom he felt standing under the multiple jets choked him up. Talk about the longest few days.

He still couldn't believe that he'd been so cocky and confident just before the shit had hit the fan. It was as if the last thirty-eight hours were a nightmare, and he couldn't wake up.

In that cell, wearing that horrible orange jumpsuit, staring at the bars, he'd had a lot of time to think about what he'd done wrong. The list went on and on but the one thing that kept slamming him in the gut was that he'd been given an opportunity for real happiness and he'd squandered it. No, that wasn't true. He'd actively tossed it away with his arrogance and mindlessness.

He hadn't been looking for it. Sure, he'd been kind of lonely, but a relationship was nowhere on his to-do list. All that had been important to him was his goddamned image. His self-righteous attitude.

The ironies had hit him hard and fast, and even now threatened to swallow him whole.

One way or another, this debacle was going to end. Drina would come through to save the day, or not. Either way, he would be checking out of Hush later today. What faced him back at the office? He had no idea. Whatever, he'd deal with it.

Not to mention that he was now the proud owner of a puppy that wasn't even house-trained. Will sighed, thinking again of Mercy, his whole body aching from lack of sleep and gut-churning remorse.

He liked her so damn much. Maybe this was what it took to wake him up. To let him see the unvarnished truth about what he'd become.

Still, it was a heavy price. One he'd be paying for years to come.

MERCY WOKE UP as someone banged on the door of the back room at PetQuarters. It took her a minute to even remember where she was, and another minute for her heart to sink as she remembered about Will. She glanced at the clock. It was after eight in the morning. "Who is it?"

"Mercy, let me in."

It was Gilly, who—true to her word—had spent the night. She'd gotten a cot from housekeeping and slept in one of the offices, even though Mercy wouldn't have minded her sharing this space.

"It's not locked. Come in."

The door burst open and Gilly, dressed in civilian clothes of a too-short skirt and a skin-tight T-shirt looked wild. She held the *New York Times* in her hand. "Look!"

She sat down next to Mercy, and shoved the second page at her.

There was a picture of Mr. and Mrs. Morris, but the story wasn't so much about them being robbed as them being robbers.

Everything Drina had told her yesterday had come to pass. The evidence was overwhelming. The Morrises had planned to bilk the insurance company and Hush out of millions, all based on lie heaped upon lie.

She thought about Drina's husband. How these same people had used the money they'd stolen from a man they'd sent to prison. All for this one giant scam.

Then her thoughts went to Will. Was everything Drina said about him true as well? Or was she trying to justify something that couldn't be justified?

"Can you believe this?" Gilly said, still too excited to sit. She hopped up and paced around the small white room. "You know Will is getting out, because it's clear he didn't do anything. All his stuff is in his room, so you know he's coming back here."

"Gilly. Stop it. Nothing's changed. Not as far as I'm concerned. I know he had his reasons, but he still lied through his teeth. I don't think I can get past that."

Her friend stopped. Her whole happy demeanor shifted into something troubling. "Really? Is that how you feel deep down?"

Mercy nodded.

After a big sigh, Gilly nodded. "Then I'm with you

a thousand percent. We all have our lines and yours was crossed. I'm just sad, though, because I have a soft spot for Will. But give me ten minutes, and I'll be hating him right along with you."

"You don't have to."

She sat again. "But I do. It's what best friends are for."

Mercy's eyes welled up, and while she shook her head at her own sentimentality, she also realized how much she appreciated Gilly. Her first true best friend. It was a huge thing, bigger than most everything else in her life.

A cell phone rang, but it wasn't Mercy's. Gilly answered as Mercy went into the bathroom to get dressed. She was just zipping her jeans when Gilly burst inside. "Hurry."

"What?"

"The police are here right now, arresting the Morrises."

Mercy put it in gear, not even sure why she wanted to be a witness. Yes, they'd lied to her, and their lies had been malicious as well as illegal. So she supposed it was only fitting that she watch them get carted away.

But there was also a tiny thought that maybe, in an act of perfect symmetry, Will would come walking into the hotel while they were walking out.

Her pace slowed as the wrongness of that image sunk in. She shouldn't be thinking redemptive thoughts about Will. He was almost as bad as the Morrises. He'd admitted it himself. He'd lied to her without a blink. Without a thought of how he would leave her broken.

Okay, so when he started the charade he hadn't planned on getting so close, but it didn't matter. It was still wrong. And selfish. And wrong.

"Will you get your ass in gear? They're going to be gone before we hit the lobby."

She finished getting dressed, washed her face in record time, and put her hair back in a ponytail. Then Gilly grabbed her and dragged her out of PetQuarters.

BY THE TIME they got downstairs, there was a nice sized crowd. Mercy had expected this, although not quite this quickly. Drina had told her she'd delivered the evidence to both the *Times* and the police, but still, she'd thought there would be a delay.

A lot of the hotel staff, in uniform and out, hovered on the perimeter of the lobby. A gazillion members of the press were there, too, and it reminded her all too much of when the movie company had been there several months ago, when that guy had been killed.

She and Gilly made their way toward the concierge desk, which wasn't all that close to the action, but was far enough away not to be caught in any pictures, either.

Mercy saw the Morrises, who didn't look so fancy now. Mrs. Morris's wig was a bit askew and she wore a dress that could best be described as frumpy. Mr. Morris had on a pretty decent pair of pants and a shirt, but his shoes were worn-out slippers. They both looked extraordinarily pissed.

Mercy wished she'd brought Lulu down to witness this. The poor dog. She deserved someone who would love her and pay attention to her. She couldn't help it if she was beautiful. Inside, she was still a puppy.

"Hey," Gilly said, poking her in the side.

Mercy looked toward the head of the throng. It was Drina. She looked elegant. Like the queen of someplace grand. Her smile was the picture of satisfaction. Mercy hadn't ever been a giant proponent of revenge, although she'd certainly considered it from time to time, but in this case, she was glad everything had turned out the way it had. With one notable exception, of course.

If only he hadn't lied. He wouldn't have even had to tell her everything. Keeping his mouth shut would have been fine.

There went her chest again. It hurt. Physically. Heartache wasn't just an expression. She ached in a way that felt permanent. Debilitating.

"Heads up," Gilly whispered, looking back toward the elevator.

Before she could have prepared herself, she saw him. Will. Not sweeping through the entrance, full of swagger and vindication, but walking slowly, looking as if he'd been beaten up. No bruises on the outside, but beaten up nonetheless.

"Ouch," Gilly said.

Mercy was thinking the same thing but not about Will. About her heart. About all that had happened. Mostly, about how in hell she was going to go on with her life when it was so painfully clear that she loved him.

THE LOBBY CLEARED considerably as the police took their prisoners outside. Will saw Drina as the parade passed her by. Her smile said it all. She'd won.

He'd gotten up an hour ago, still exhausted but unable to sleep. They'd delivered the *Times* and as he'd sipped his first cup of coffee, he'd read the article twice. Drina had assured him that everything would turn out, but in the back of his mind he hadn't believed it. Once again, she'd shown him that she was not to be underestimated.

Even he hadn't suspected fraud of this magnitude. The insurance adjuster was going down, as was the diamond expert who'd falsified the appraisal. It was the kind of scandal the public loved, and he was quite sure it would sell one hell of a lot of papers.

He still wasn't sure how the courts were going to feel about his part in all this. He'd have to come up with something to explain turning himself in for a crime he hadn't committed.

It didn't matter. He doubted even the most cunning attorneys would be able to connect this all back to Drina. So she was in the clear. And so was Mercy.

He headed for his grandmother. The closer he got, the younger she looked. This, he supposed, was her way of keeping Marius alive. She'd gotten her revenge, all right, and he supposed she deserved to revel.

"I see the attorney got you out," she said. "I'm glad. I would have hated for you to miss this."

"You did it. You pulled it off."

"It hurts me that you suspected anything less."

"I won't make that mistake again."

Drina put her hand on his arm. "Don't worry. I'm through. I'm going back to the house, to the garden and the card games. No more."

"I'll sleep better."

She shook her head. "No, you won't. You'll worry about your business and your reputation. Now you'll have to explain to all your society friends why you turned yourself in. It won't be easy for you."

"I don't care. I don't have the energy to worry about it."

"That's because there's something more important. Have you spoken to her?"

"What's the point?"

"William, haven't you learned anything? Go. Try. Do whatever you have to do. It took me years to get back at them for Marius. Years. But I didn't give up."

"She has every reason to hate me."

"Give her reasons to love you."

He kissed his grandmother on the cheek, hoping *their* relationship, at least, could be repaired. As for Mercy? He couldn't see it. It was time to check out. He'd go up, pack his bags. Then he'd get Buster from PetQuarters.

Buster. He'd decided to keep the dog. It was probably just another stupid move on his part, but he couldn't bear to part with the little guy, not after all they'd been through. He just wished…

Screw it. There was no use wishing.

MERCY WAS IN Buster's suite, watching as he chewed on a bone that was almost his size. All of a sudden, she had three dogs to worry about. Lulu, Pumpkin and Buster.

She was going to need to find them homes. Buster and Lulu wouldn't be a problem. Pumpkin? Not so easy. The one thing she knew for sure was that she wasn't going to abandon the little Chihuahua. No way she would turn any of them over to a shelter, even a no-kill. They deserved better. They deserved love. And trust.

She wouldn't look out there. The staff was all abuzz

about the arrest, about Will's innocence, but he wasn't innocent, was he? He'd lied. She didn't really know anything about him, except that he was a liar. And that he had a family that was as screwed up as her own.

"I live in SoHo."

Mercy froze as his voice washed over her. He was right there, right outside the cage.

"I've never even been in Wichita. I don't have a nephew. Just my grandmother. Probably a whole bunch of other relatives, but I haven't seen any of them in years. For what it's worth, I never met the Cristescus. Or maybe I did, but it would have been years ago."

"It's not helping," she said.

"I have a company. A successful one. I do travel a lot, that part was true. I don't have a serious relationship in my life. Hadn't wanted one. Didn't expect to become attached to anyone, let alone a pet concierge."

"I'm not listening."

"I'm going to take Buster home with me. I have a little yard in the back. I figure he won't care that it's small because he's small. I'll find someone to stay with him when I'm on the road. Someone good."

Mercy put her head in her hands. The one part of him that she could count on, that she knew beyond doubt, was that he lied like a son of a bitch. He was fabulous at it, and how stupid would she be to let him take her in again?

"I have money. I collect modern art. I use a company plane that I lease with several other CEOs. I never thought about having children because I figured I'd be a lousy father. And I love you."

"Stop it. Just…"

"I will. I promise. Only not until I tell you again that

I'm sorry. I had something remarkable happen, and I blew it because I'm a born con man. I conned you. No doubt about it. It was easier. That's all. I didn't have to think about it. Before I got to know you, you were a mark. Most people I've met in my life are marks. It's a problem. A big one. It won't be easy to change. I'd have to want to change really badly. Because people don't like to change unless something huge is at stake. Like losing you."

She wasn't looking at him. Her focus was on Buster. On his little tail, his little nose. She wasn't even really listening, because why should she.

Only, Buster wasn't chewing on the big bone anymore. He was over at the side of the cage, jumping up and down, outbarking Pumpkin in an attempt to get to his Uncle Will.

Mercy stood up and opened the suite door. Buster ran as fast as his little legs could carry him until he'd found his objective. Will picked him up and Buster could hardly contain his excitement.

She walked to the next suite, Pumpkin's. Mercy opened that door, too. Pumpkin shot straight at Will. Barking like crazy. The next suite was Lulu's and after that was Chance's. Mercy opened up every single suite door. Then she went to the middle pen, and she let out the two dogs that were in there.

Every single dog had gone straight for Will. Except for Rio, who had lumbered to her side. She put her hand on his head as she watched.

Of course, it could just mean that the dogs were attracted to the other dogs. Yeah. Buster was excited, Pumpkin was barky. It wasn't Will. This was all stupid.

Whether dogs liked him or not had nothing to do with the fact that he'd lied through his teeth. About everything. About most things.

"So I was wondering," Will said, holding Buster up so the dog's tongue was a safe distance away. "If we could try this whole thing again. I mean, Buster, he needs a lot of training. And I need a lot of practice at telling the truth. I wouldn't expect things to change overnight. I mean, you'd need a lot of evidence that I could, in fact, tell the truth. Consistently. If you'd, you know, consider it."

She looked at him, which was her big mistake. Because she wasn't just remembering the lies. She was remembering how his lips felt. How he'd clucked like a chicken. How he made her laugh and smile and how her heart ached thinking about not seeing him again.

"I can't," she said. "I've got to find homes for Lulu and Pumpkin."

"Well, I can help you with that," he said, taking a tentative step toward her.

"How?"

"Well, they're all pretty small. I'm sure they'd all be fine in my little yard."

"Three dogs. You'd take in three dogs. Including Pumpkin."

He walked toward her, trailing a whole gang of dogs. When he was close, when the dogs had swarmed around them both, he looked into her eyes. "I'd take in three hundred."

"No lying," she said.

He nodded slowly. Carefully.

"Not even little white lies."

"Not even if you ask me if your butt looks big in some dress."

She couldn't help her smile. "Well, let's not get crazy."

"So this is yes? You'll let me try again? The real me?"

Mercy knew she was taking a giant chance. He could hurt her so badly. But he could also make her so happy. "This is yes," she said.

A moment later, Buster was barking at Pumpkin, who was barking at Lulu, who was yapping at Rio. And Mercy? She was being kissed.

* * * * *

THOROUGHBRED LEGACY
*The stakes are high when it comes to love,
horse racing, family secrets
and broken promises.*

*A new exciting Harlequin continuity series coming
soon!*
Led by New York Times *bestselling author
Elizabeth Bevarly*
FLIRTING WITH TROUBLE

Here's a preview!

THE DOOR CLOSED behind them, throwing them into darkness and leaving them utterly alone. And the next thing Daniel knew, he heard himself saying, "Marnie, I'm sorry about the way things turned out in Del Mar."

She said nothing at first, only strode across the room and stared out the window beside him. Although he couldn't see her well in the darkness—he still hadn't switched on a light…but then, neither had she—he imagined her expression was a little preoccupied, a little anxious, a little confused.

Finally, very softly, she said, "Are you?"

He nodded, then, worried she wouldn't be able to see the gesture, added, "Yeah. I am. I should have said goodbye to you."

"Yes, you should have."

Actually, he thought, there were a lot of things he should have done in Del Mar. He'd had *a lot* riding on the Pacific Classic, and even more on his entry, Little Joe, but after meeting Marnie, the Pacific Classic had been the last thing on Daniel's mind. His loss at Del Mar had pretty much ended his career before it had even begun, and he'd had to start all over again, rebuilding from nothing.

He simply had not then and did not now have room in his life for a woman as potent as Marnie Roberts. He was a horseman first and foremost. From the time he was a schoolboy, he'd known what he wanted to do with his life—be the best possible trainer he could be.

He had to make sure Marnie understood—and he understood, too—why things had ended the way they had eight years ago. He just wished he could find the words to do that. Hell, he wished he could find the *thoughts* to do that.

"You made me forget things, Marnie, things that I really needed to remember. And that scared the hell out of me. Little Joe should have won the Classic. He was by far the best horse entered in that race. But I didn't give him the attention he needed and deserved that week, because all I could think about was you. Hell, when I woke up that morning all I wanted to do was lie there and look at you, and then wake you up and make love to you again. If I hadn't left when I did—the way I did—I might still be lying there in that bed with you, thinking about nothing else."

"And would that be so terrible?" she asked.

"Of course not," he told her. "But that wasn't why I was in Del Mar," he repeated. "I was in Del Mar to win a race. That was my job. And my work was the most important thing to me."

She said nothing for a moment, only studied his face in the darkness as if looking for the answer to a very important question. Finally she asked, "And what's the most important thing to you now, Daniel?"

Wasn't the answer to that obvious? "My work," he answered automatically.

She nodded slowly. "Of course," she said softly. "That is, after all, what you do best."

Her comment, too, puzzled him. She made it sound as if being good at what he did was a bad thing.

She bit her lip thoughtfully, her eyes fixed on his, glimmering in the scant moonlight that was filtering through the window. And damned if Daniel didn't find himself wanting to pull her into his arms and kiss her. But as much as it might have felt as if no time had passed since Del Mar, there were eight years between now and then. And eight years was a long time in the best of circumstances. For Daniel and Marnie, it was virtually a lifetime.

So Daniel turned and started for the door, then halted. He couldn't just walk away and leave things as they were, unsettled. He'd done that eight years ago and regretted it.

"It *was* good to see you again, Marnie," he said softly. And since he was being honest, he added, "I hope we see each other again."

She didn't say anything in response, only stood silhouetted against the window with her arms wrapped around her in a way that made him wonder whether she was doing it because she was cold, or if she just needed something—someone—to hold on to. In either case, Daniel understood. There was an emptiness clinging to him that he suspected would be there for a long time.

* * * * *

THOROUGHBRED LEGACY
coming soon wherever books are sold!

Thoroughbred Legacy

Launching in June 2008

A dramatic new 12-book continuity that embodies the American Dream.

Meet the Prestons, owners of Quest Stables, a successful horse-racing and breeding empire. But the lives, loves and reputations of this hardworking family are put at risk when a breeding scandal unfolds.

Flirting with Trouble

by New York Times **bestselling author**

ELIZABETH BEVARLY

Eight years ago, publicist Marnie Roberts spent seven days of bliss with Australian horse trainer Daniel Whittleson. But just as quickly, he disappeared. Now Marnie is heading to Australia to finally confront the man she's never been able to forget.

The stakes are high when it comes to love, horse racing, family secrets and broken promises.

A new exciting Harlequin continuity series coming soon!

www.eHarlequin.com

REQUEST YOUR FREE BOOKS!

2 FREE NOVELS
PLUS 2
FREE GIFTS!

Red-hot reads!

YES! Please send me 2 FREE Harlequin® Blaze™ novels and my 2 FREE gifts (gifts are worth about $10). After receiving them, if I don't wish to receive any more books, I can return the shipping statement marked "cancel". If I don't cancel, I will receive 6 brand-new novels every month and be billed just $4.24 per book in the U.S. or $4.71 per book in Canada, plus 25¢ shipping and handling per book and applicable taxes, if any*. That's a savings of 15% or more off the cover price! I understand that accepting the 2 free books and gifts places me under no obligation to buy anything. I can always return a shipment and cancel at any time. Even if I never buy another book, the two free books and gifts are mine to keep forever.

151 HDN ERVA 351 HDN ERUX

Name	(PLEASE PRINT)	
Address		Apt. #
City	State/Prov.	Zip/Postal Code

Signature (if under 18, a parent or guardian must sign)

Mail to the Harlequin Reader Service:
IN U.S.A.: P.O. Box 1867, Buffalo, NY 14240-1867
IN CANADA: P.O. Box 609, Fort Erie, Ontario L2A 5X3

Not valid to current subscribers of Harlequin Blaze books.

Want to try two free books from another line?
Call 1-800-873-8635 or visit www.morefreebooks.com.

* Terms and prices subject to change without notice. N.Y. residents add applicable sales tax. Canadian residents will be charged applicable provincial taxes and GST. This offer is limited to one order per household. All orders subject to approval. Credit or debit balances in a customer's account(s) may be offset by any other outstanding balance owed by or to the customer. Please allow 4 to 6 weeks for delivery. Offer available while quantities last.

Your Privacy: Harlequin Books is committed to protecting your privacy. Our Privacy Policy is available online at www.eHarlequin.com or upon request from the Reader Service. From time to time we make our lists of customers available to reputable third parties who may have a product or service of interest to you. If you would prefer we not share your name and address, please check here. ☐

HB08

Silhouette®

Desire

Royal Seductions

Michelle Celmer delivers a powerful miniseries in
Royal Seductions; where two brothers fight for the
crown and discover love. In _The King's Convenient Bride_,
the king discovers his marriage of convenience to the
woman he's been promised to wed is turning all too
real. The playboy prince proposes a mock engagement
to defuse rumors circulating about him and restore
order to the kingdom…until his pretend fiancée
becomes pregnant in _The Illegitimate Prince's Baby_.

Look for

THE KING'S CONVENIENT BRIDE
&
THE ILLEGITIMATE PRINCE'S BABY

BY MICHELLE CELMER

Available in June 2008 wherever you buy books.

Always Powerful, Passionate and Provocative.

HARLEQUIN®

Blaze™

COMING NEXT MONTH

#399 CROSSING THE LINE Lori Wilde
Perfect Anatomy

Confidential Rejuvenations, an exclusive Texas boutique clinic, has a villain on the loose. But it's the new surgeon, Dr. Dante Nash, who is getting the most attention from chief nurse Elle Kingston....

#400 THE LONER Rhonda Nelson
Men Out of Uniform

Lucas "Huck" Finn is thrilled to join Ranger Security—until he learns his new job is to babysit Sapphira Stravos, a doggie-toting debutante. Still, he knows there's more to Sapphira than meets the eye. And what's meeting the eye is damn hard to resist.

#401 NOBODY DOES IT BETTER Jennifer LaBrecque
Lust in Translation

Gage Carswell, British spy, is all about getting his man—or in this case, his woman. He's after Holly Smith, whom he believes to be a notorious agent. And he's willing to do anything—squire her around Venice, play out all her sexual fantasies—to achieve his goal. Too bad this time *his* woman isn't the *right* woman.

#402 SLOW HANDS Leslie Kelly
The Wrong Bed: Again and Again

Heiress Madeleine Turner only wants to stop her stepmother from making a huge mistake. That's how she ends up buying Jake Wallace at a charity bachelor auction. But now that she's won the sexy guy, what's she going to do with him? Lucky for her, Jake has a few ideas....

#403 SEX BY THE NUMBERS Marie Donovan
Blush

Accountant—undercover! Pretending to be seriously sexy Dane Weiss's ditsy personal assistant to secretly hunt for missing company funds isn't what Keeley Davis signed up for. But the overtime is out of this world!

#404 BELOW THE BELT Sarah Mayberry

Jamie Sawyer wants to redeem her family name in the boxing world. To do that, she needs trainer Cooper Fitzgerald. Spending time together ignites a sizzling attraction...one he's resisting. Looks as if she'll have to aim her best shots a little low to get what she wants.